TERRY CLARK

None But The Righteous

First edition

Editing by Gregory Hedgepeth
Editing by Sacha Hamilton

This book was professionally typeset on Reedsy.
Find out more at reedsy.com

Contents

Preface

These stories are a culmination of the sights, sounds and life (particularly Black life) in Lawndale. One commonality in all of these stories is the setting. Each story takes place on the Westside of Chicago, specifically Lawndale and Austin. These stories reflect some of my personal childhood experiences, teenage years and ultimately as an adult. I have been a Westsider all of my life. Consequently, I also have tried to infuse each story with imaginative realities, dialogue, cultural nuances, characters and setting. Hopefully, they speak with their own language, practicality and magic.

Acknowledgement

These following stories were previously published:

"None But The Righteous" in *New Scriptor* (a forum for Illinois educators), Vol. XII

"The Preacher's Wife" in *Taj Mahal Review*

"Sonnyman" in *Expressions from Englewood*

"Sonnyman" in *Taj Mahal Review*

"JT's Song" in *Art & Prose Magazine* (an e-zine), Vol. 1—No. 8

"Little Rogue" in *Expressions from Englewood*

"Evil in the World" in *Taj Mahal Review*

Dedication

This book is dedicated to so many people. I really don't know where to begin.

First and foremost, I thank God for giving me life and my parents, Albert and Susie Clark, who taught their children to give rather than take. Thank you. My brothers, some of whom have passed on—Randy, *never without a book!* Percy and Tomie. Patrick (the *real* musician!) and my sisters, Shirley and Annie. My great-niece and nephews who put up with me and my ways: Nicole (Jaidyn & Joshua), Stephanie, Jr. (Gabe) and Elder Willie J. Sams.

My journey has brought me in contact with so many good people: Professor Sam Michaelson (you brought me to Baldwin and sent me into teaching). Professor Vertreace-Doody, your feedback has been invaluable. Professors Cromley and Junious (creativity speaks; we listen). The Communications faculty/staff (we laugh much too much!). Dr. Ellis (*write what you feel*). Editor-in-Chief Gregory Hedgepeth and Lead Editor Sasha Hamilton for making this whole thing happen!

Stephanie, my heart. I know—I talk too much and too long... your gentle way of telling me to shut up... *thank you.*

Other people I would like to thank: Karl and Linda Brinson,

Robert Townsend, Professor Angela Jackson, Dennis Olive, Deacon John Green, Jackie Elkins, Thelma Griffin, Eugene Hamilton, Yakub Dosumnu, J. J. McCormick, Earline Williams, Judith Starks, Dr. Jennifer Hunt, Desmond McFarlane, Leslie Jones, David Buchanan, James Buchanan, Arletta Walker, Michelle Buchannan, Gerald and Teresa Floyd, John and Debbie Fallahay, Michael and Valerie Watkins, Kenneth Vick, Karl Vick, The Q-Street Boys, Prentice Jackson, Fritz Bush, Dr. Robert Cruthird and Professor Jeanette Williams, DC Randle, Ron and Karla Williams, Professors Corey and Julie Hall, Dr. Jeff Sellen, Edward Brownlee, Rudolph Henry and Leonard Wash.

None But The Righteous

What makes us whole sometimes can take several lifetimes—we search and might fall to Earth too soon. Some call it a journey. Others call it a trip. Its movement grows and grows. Sometimes it manifests itself through ritual and ceremony and for Miles the time had come. He would become three dollars, six dimes. He could no longer avoid his destiny.

A ringing old school gospel spiritual filled the corridor and outer halls. Its rhythmic power stretched out its hands and guided the swaying congregation. The sacred words and melody emanating from the sacred mouths of the congregation reverberated and echoed in Miles' ears and opened them like the mouth of the ocean. He smiled nervously and peered through and around the pillars of creased, stiffened black suit pants and starched white dresses.

For Miles, excitement and fright intermingled with the heavily perfumed air. Although he frowned, he secretly loved the way the sisters hugged and buried his head between their breasts when they greeted him and the other young children. The experience always left a lump in his pants.

Wide eyed and fascinated, the scene of baptism made the hair on the back of his neck stand on end. He had badgered Noah and Darlene the last two weeks, asking questions about their

1

pending event—what it would be like to reach out and take the right hand of God. Questions filled the pool in his mind. Did He have big hands? Fingers? Or, were they as soft and soothing as his mother's? What if God didn't accept their hands?

"He'll take it!" Noah insisted every time Miles asked and then shooed him away from him and his friends. The last two years, Miles had seen several other children his age baptized. But he did not know the children very well and was too shy to approach them.

The congregation swayed, its holy fury gaining momentum with every movement. The outside world had shut down. No one, no one, but the righteous could bear witness and understand. In the midst of the shouting, in the early morning service, Reverend Martin had gotten on a roll about how Jesus would come back like a thief in the middle of the night, and that his face would appear in the window, scarred and bleeding, feeling sorry for us and all the rest of mankind. At times, this shook Miles up pretty badly. How come Noah and Darlene never got scared? Miles often sat through the services with a million pictures of kingdom come running through his mind.

Miles moved off to the side of the basement. He carefully avoided the smatterings of water from the pool and the high humidity of summer's work. The face peering in through the broken, stained glass window startled him momentarily. It was only Mr. Griot from down the street. He was well known around the neighborhood and thought of as crazy. Miles just thought him to be different. Parents warned their kids all the time to keep away. Even Darlene and Noah drew back. Griot fascinated and teased Miles' curiosity. Sometimes, while hiding on the side of Griot's house, Miles hung on every overheard note of music and prophetic, mysterious word. Griot stood, knees bent—hunched over a circle of bones, a large bowl of water and wilted flower petals that floated on its surface. Griot sprinkled blue dust, spinning around in semi-circles. He stopped and leaned his head back and upward. His breathing was heavy. His chest moved up and down through his green fatigue jacket. The heavy breathing stopped. Griot lowered himself on his knees. He gently thrust his hands forward, letting go the last of the petals and powder. Then suddenly, he turned around towards the window. His eyes locked with Miles', whose heart jumped ten feet. He lost his balance and he fell off the rickety garbage can he teetered on. Miles heard Griot laughing, but was too afraid to turn around and look back. He kept on running down the street until he reached home.

Everyone would rush past Griot with his bottles and bags. Miles' mother would say his clothes "were rumpled but clean." Word was that ever since his wife passed away, his mind had gone with her. Griot's wife had long been a member of the church and had died several years earlier. People felt that when she was still around, she took care of him. She understood him in ways no one else could. The parishioners felt for her, being attached to someone like him. Whenever one of the sisters would offer her hand in prayer, Griot's wife would smile and give a knowing look. Confused, the sister would fan herself, shake her head in disbelief and change the subject. Even the funeral arrangements Mr. Griot made for her rankled the pastor and congregation— "some kind of African mess," he called it.

Most times, Mr. Griot knew how to stay away. It made Reverend Martin nervous when he would suddenly show up in a Sunday morning service, sitting, fidgeting in the last row of the sanctuary. Griot's penetrating eyes, sunken and graying always felt too close. The congregation had finally banned him from any board meetings or committees. He asked too many questions they said, and nobody wanted to listen to his long-winded speeches. By the time Griot would be done, the food on the table had started to get cold. Griot's home was a virtual, antique ritual, filled with African art, old army souvenirs and brown, dusty newspapers stacked high into an arching ceiling.

Miles turned his attention from Griot to the ceremony about to begin. He could not figure out how Noah and Darlene would feel when they went under water, especially with the reverend hollering at the top of his lungs. First Darlene—down she went. Miles gulped and swallowed his spit. Reverend Martin, short in stature, but solidly built, threw his tiny head back and flung it from left to right with his eyes closed tightly. Then, Reverend Martin bucked his gray eyes and swiveled his head in rhythm with his cadenced speech. The standing congregation, now whipped into a sanctified frenzy, shouted "Amen!" in unison, as Miles' chest heaved upward and then lowered itself. His eyes followed Darlene and he thought she would drown.Reverend Martin held her down so long, he thought. It seemed the Reverend brought her up for air just in time.

"Hallelujah!" Darlene's mother screamed, raising her arms and hands into the air before falling into a foot-stomping holy dance, shuffling to her own secret beat. She caught and clutched her hat as it slid down her head. Her heavy round, squat torso moved by her short, thick legs never missed a beat. She had sweated through her short sleeve dress. The stains were big and round. Miles worried that she would slip and fall onto the sky-blue painted concrete floor. But she never fell, never slipped. The hands of the Holy Ghost guided her movements, as she danced and weaved through the congregation speaking in tongues. Each member respectfully stepped out of the way, urging her on. A member of the usher board slowly trailed her, whispering her own sweet dialogue, fanning, smiling and nodding her head in affirmation. Miles' heart beat faster. He loosened his tie, but wouldn't dare take it off completely. That would be blaspheming on a Sunday. He watched as Darlene lifted her long slim dark brown legs and stepped from the pool, clad in only a drenched T-shirt. With a swiftness that startled Miles, several members of the Mothers Board rushed forward, surrounding and smothering Darlene with towels. Miles gawked at the pointed nipples he never knew Darlene had, protruding through her drenched clothing. Her toenails sparkled in the puddle she had made, before being whisked away by the Mothers.

The congregation proclaimed, "Amen! Amen! And Amen again!" Darlene was only three years older than him. Taller and skinnier, but wiry and strong enough to beat him up whenever he said something smart to her. She was tough, but being born the second child of three and sandwiched between two boys was sometimes like having a clown to the left and a joker to the right. Darlene held her own though. Often, when there was a fight brewing between Noah and one of the other boys on the block, the sight of Darlene storming down the street would make the offender think twice about carrying out his threats—he'd rather deal with Noah.

The Reverend had segued into another pre-baptismal sermon, imploring the skeptical congregation that Noah was ready and next. Noah stood solemn and quiet, staring straight ahead, not moving. Noah was taller than the Reverend, so he had to look down on him, while Reverend Martin looked up into his eyes. He had told Miles the evening before, while they sat and watched TV in the living room that he wasn't scared and that he'd know just how to act when the reverend called his number.

"All I gotta do is hold my breath—just like taking a swim!" Noah bragged and strutted with his hands on his hips, back and forth between Miles and the TV.

Their mother overheard and called out from the kitchen, "Boy, you gon' get yourself in a whole mess of trouble you keep talking like that!" The warning silenced Noah and Miles. They covered their mouths and laughed inwardly, turning their attention back to the black and white picture tube, flickering in the half-lit living room. Darlene stuck her head through her bedroom doorway and pointed an "*I told you so*" finger at both of them.

Miles craned his neck and tried to catch Noah's eyes to see if he was scared, but by then, Noah had turned his back to the audience. Reverend Martin reached up and held his shoulders with his big, broad brown hands. He whispered his hot breath directly into Noah's ears, the same way he did with Darlene. Noah nodded his head at every word. Then, Noah lowered his head and closed his eyes. Miles' imagination took off. What was he saying to Noah? And when his time came, would he say the same to him?

Reverend Martin turned to the congregation and announced, "He's ready!" To Noah, "Are you ready?"

"I'm ready," Noah whispered back with his head bowed.

Reverend Martin' fingers squeezed his bony shoulders again, "Don't make a liar out of me, boy! Are you ready?"

Noah drew his breath. "I'm ready!" he shouted in his loudest voice with conviction to the congregation and whoever was listening.

They walked up the four wooden stairs, stepped over the side and down the concrete stairs into the blue pool. Miles held his breath and wondered if Noah was ready. Three times Reverend

Martin dunked him, saying in best preacher's voice: "Do you believe?"

Each time he went under, Miles covered his eyes with his hands. When he took them down, he tried in vain to see if Noah was okay. Miles looked up at their mother. She was crying and wringing her hands and mouthing words in a language he didn't understand. Miles concluded that since she hadn't tried to rescue Noah, he must be okay. Noah was breathing hard and trying to catch his breath.

Later, he and Miles stood in the small bathroom while Noah dried himself. "Was you scared, Noah?"

"Naw ain't nothing to it. Three dollars, six dimes. You just got to be ready. That's why Reverend Martin kept asking me that over and over again. Didn't you know?"

"I thought..." His words lingered, but Noah was quickly dressed in his Sunday suit again and out of the door.

Miles put his questions to the side when he stepped out into the hall and smelled the homemade biscuits, dressing, chicken and turkey. After each baptizing, there would be a celebration of the renewal of the soul. The honorees were seated at the head table with Reverend Martin and the other pastors. His mother had saved him a seat next to her. She patted the chair and Miles sat. She still sweated from the excitement of the ceremony. Their mother, Sister Wayne, eyes still moist with tears, smiled through them, humming the same song she brewed each morning in the kitchen with her coffee. The scent of her perfume, mixed with perspiration and make-up, ran up and into Miles' nose. It didn't take him away from the task at hand. He indulged himself with every mouthful that went down. His mother gently dabbed her face. Then, in the middle of a chicken wing, his worst fears materialized. Reverend Martin made his way over to the table while making his rounds.

"Well now, young man, I 'spect I'll be seeing you pretty soon. What do you say? You think you ready to cross over? Don't say so if you ain't now."

That last piece of chicken got stuck. Miles tried hard to swallow but couldn't. He looked up pleadingly at his mother. His eyes said, "Mama, please don't ..." It did no good. She was already basking in the light.

"Oh, Reverend, say no more. I'll have him ready." She was excited. First, Noah and now Miles? Just the way she planned it.

"That's all right, Sister Wayne. Just make sure he's ready. He got to be ready!" The Reverend got up and continued his trek down the table and the waiting hands. Miles stared straight ahead. His heart started to beat fast again. He became angry on the inside. He hadn't asked for this.

* * *

Monday morning rushed in like a lightning strike. Miles hadn't slept much. Childhood and summer vacation should have been important. The air of anticipation, images of picnics, of barbecue, of holiday antics, of fire crackers and colorful sparklers usually danced in Miles' mind at this time of the year. It was days before the Fourth of July. But this time, Miles' impending ceremony occupied his moves.

As Darlene, Noah and mama slept through an early light, the morning continued to open its eyes with a lull. The summer's heat had already ascended upon the humid and sweaty streets of Lawndale.

Across the street in Douglas Park, a few children had started their summer revelries. Several played next to the rite of passage tree, whose branches and leaves, watched them from up on high. Very few of Miles' friends had the nerve to climb it. If one did, he would be granted the title of king, sit in between the limbs that had grown and branched off into a V-shaped nest from the trunk, giving orders to his subjects on the ground.

Miles leaned against the window in the living room that faced the park and blew his breath against it. He practiced writing words before the fan made the letters fade into the air. He heard his mother's footsteps, as she headed towards the bathroom and then the kitchen. He just wanted her around. He licked his lips, hoping that she was off work today and heading for the kitchen to start the morning breakfast.

The Preacher's Wife (Nothing But the Hand of God)

Lucille sat, hardly able to breathe, sweating though her clothes in the interrogation room off to the side of the squad room. The ninety-degree weather outside was not nice. Detective Heathrow felt Lucille deserved the treatment. No air-conditioning. No air movement. Just stale and suffocating air. The window in the room was left closed on purpose. Sweat soaked through her rose-colored sundress. Lucille wiped her brow with a dingy handkerchief she had found at the bottom of her purse and sighed, wondering what Lil' Willie would think.

She already knew what Reverend Powers would say. "Woe unto those who don't obey!" he'd preach, pointing his chafed, dry scolding index finger in her direction. "Obey! Obey! Obey!"

It all came with the package. The marriage. A boy, more influenced by his daddy than his mother. The boy was the worst. He took after the old man totally. Wore his clothes like him. Even began to walk and talk like him. Lucille hung her head and quickly swirled her finger from right to left in a circular motion to speak her mind and mood, "Whoooo!"

Willie was only three when she first saw the signs one morning at the breakfast table.

"Eat your oatmeal. Don't play in it. Come. Be a big boy for Mama," Lucille purred like a woman trying to seduce a grown man.

Lil' Willie wouldn't fall for it. "No!" he screamed violently, throwing his spoon against the kitchen wall. The force of the spoon marked the light-yellow paint for twenty-five years. Like the cold wound Hezekiah had already put on her heart, Lil' Willie's scorn only festered, grew larger and burned itself into the spot.

Each time Lucille mentioned painting over it, Hezekiah would berate her. "Had no business making Lil' Willie angry. You just mess things up and don't know how to fix 'em."

As he got older, Willie started to dress like Hezekiah, who always looked like he was on his way to a funeral. Dark suit and tie. Polished, black or brown shoes. Even on the weekdays, in the middle of the day he would dress like that. Lucille often wondered how Lil' Willie would ever go to school and play with the other children and get dirty like them. It was almost as if Lil' Willie knew from day one that he would get preferential treatment from his teachers and the rest of the administration.

Over the years, Lil' Willie never changed his style of dress and even skipped gym. Being the preacher's son had its perks. So Lil' Willie made it point to carry his Bible everywhere he went. It made it easier to make people think he was deep in thought about scripture. The Mothers Board acknowledged early on that they approved of his growth and development and smothered him with their perfume, big hugs and big breasts. Every woman with a daughters wanted to get on Lil' Willie's good side, in order to make the route just that much easier to Hezekiah's pants. By sixteen, Lil' Willie was no longer little and practically married off to every teenaged female member in the congregation. Much like this father, Willie father took complete advantage of the situation, dating several young ladies at the same time, never committing to just one.

Through the window on the door, Lucille saw Detective Heathrow out in the squad room, sitting on the edge of his desk. The room was busy with activity as the other officers darted throughout. Lucille wondered whether Heathrow had discussed her case with the other officer he faced or if they were talking about the baseball game. Was she more interesting than the Cubs? They couldn't be all that interesting. Each year, they started out with high hopes of winning a pennant or at least being in contention in September, but it never seemed to happen. Same old stuff. Same old play. Same old fans. Maybe Ms. Kiwi could help. At least she had given them something to talk about, she mused. A preacher's wife? A simple trip and fall? A bullet to the heart? Lucille was sure the coroner wouldn't have to search long to find the cause of death. Maybe Willie would preach the funeral. Yes, that would be nice. It was the least he could do since he loved him so much. Loved him so much. Loved him so much!

Lucille tried to love Hezekiah too. Tried very hard to be a good, long-suffering first lady. Hezekiah's creed was that she should, always "obey." Obey his every command and never question it, or else she would get the belt and she wouldn't want that. If it came to that, Lucille's self-esteem would kick in and she would cry. Not because she felt the hard, hot, stinging licks, but because she felt that she had let Hezekiah down and did not fulfill her obligations as a wife.

The beatings would always end the same, a hot bath to keep the swelling down and a gentle scolding by Hezekiah. "Lucille, baby, why you wannna make me mad? Don't you know Daddy don't like to put the hurt on you? When Daddy has to do that, it don't make me feel good." Hezekiah rubbed Lucille's back as she wept in heaving breaths. Lil' Willie always listened quietly on the other side of the door. Hezekiah closed his eyes and threw back his head, sucking air between his teeth. "Lord made y'all from Adam's rib. That mean you ain't 'exactly whole, you see. So you'll need us to get along. You follow, Lucy?"

In a twisted way, Lucille loved the way Hezekiah called her "Lucy." Lustful and commanding was how the name had come to wrap itself around Lucille's mind and heart. There was no turning back. No leaving the fold. When Lucille's father gave Hezekiah her hand in marriage, she didn't know that she was jumping from the frying pan and into the fire. Her father had always warned her as she grew up.

"Gal, you got to find yourself a man. If you don't your hair gon' be all over the floor before you twenty-one. And if that happens, we'll be the embarrassment of the neighborhood! Once you leave, don't come back. You can't do no better than a preacher!"

"No better than a preacher." Lucille silently mouthed the words to herself. *Did they leave me in this room with the windows shut on purpose or did they forget that I needed to breathe?* Breathing on a regular basis was something Lucille had to do when she could. Being Hezekiah's wife was not the easiest thing in the world. He was the reason her hair was coming out, not because she couldn't find a man. Lord have mercy, she had lost her mind.

Lucille felt the heat overtake her. She began to nod and kept flinging her head backwards to stay awake.

Shouldn't I be more concerned? Lucille thought. *This is serious business.* After all, a man had died. A man who was her husband, a father, a brother, a son. Only a husband to her and what a husband. Reverend Powers had been born into the ministry. In his grandfather's footsteps, he had started preaching when he was eight years old. The fire and brimstone burned in his young, innocent eyes. Unlike Lucille and the other children, Hezekiah was always in the scripture and quick with a lecture when his peers did wrong. But Lucille had grown to know something else. Something other people didn't know. Over the years, she had learned the hard way that with the pedestal and the pulpit come privilege. Six months before their marriage, Hezekiah claimed he had to make sure Lucille was still a virgin.

"You know I don't want to get to that night of consummation and find out something different. The Bible says..."

"Why can't you just take my word for it?" Lucille interrupted. "Don't you trust me?" Lucille played with the curled, black bangs that hung just above her shoulders.

Hezekiah insisted. "This is what my father required of my mother. It's also a test to see if you will obey."

His eyebrows widened and rose as he placed his hand on Lucille's breast. Lucille tried to resist, but she gave in that night. She couldn't turn down the opportunity to marry the one man all of the church girls in town were chasing. The one man whom mothers would have gladly sacrificed their daughters for at Hezekiah's feet. Lucille got her golden apple and then some.

Lucille was startled by Detective Heathrow's sudden entry into the room. He held a balled up napkin with ketchup stains in his hand.

"Lunch must have been good," Lucille said teasingly.

Detective Heathrow was not amused. "Listen, lady, here's what we have and here's what we know. Apparently, it was the fall down a flight of stairs. Internal bleeding explains the lack of blood spill. No sign of struggle. Did you push him from behind?"

Lucille protested, "I didn't..."

Detective Heathrow cut her off and pounded his fist into the center of the table. "Well, how in the hell did it happen? And don't give me that lame ass story about Miss Kiwi or whatever her name is. You're the only suspect. Your son was at school. You and Reverend Powers were at home alone. Or were you? Did that lady help? You two got something going on? Tell me the truth!"

Lucille inhaled her breath and started whimpering. Heathrow's brow furled and his eyes rolled toward the ceiling. He felt a twinge of empathy for Lucille and decided to take a softer approach.

"Tell me about this Miss Kiwi. Did she put you up to it or what?"

Lucille stopped crying. She let out a breath and fanned under the hem of her sun dress. "Miss Kiwi... Miss Kiwi, she—a friend of mine in the congregation referred me to her. She said Miss Kiwi had helped her before, maybe she could help me. She gave me the number and address. I called the number and set up an appointment. She told me to come that afternoon."

* * *

Hezekiah and Lil' Willie had gone. It was eleven o'clock and Lucille rushed around the house the rest of the morning. She finished cooking dinner, covered the plates in aluminum foil and placed them in the refrigerator. Lucille checked her purse, making sure all the money was there. Miss Kiwi emphasized, several times to her, that any advice given would not be as reliable if she didn't bring the exact amount. As she hurried towards the door, she stopped to look back at the clock on the mantel to make sure of the time. It looked as if it were frozen, yet still ticking, stuck on eleven o'clock. *It should be later than that,* Lucille thought.

Lucille got off of the bus at Wabash and Randolph. She walked slowly, checking the addresses on the huge office buildings. There, in the window of the second floor of 132 N. Wabash was a lighted, neon sign that read *Readings by Kiwi.* Lucille rushed and entered through the revolving doors. The cool, air-conditioned breeze cleared her nostrils. She acknowledged the greetings of the security guard at the desk and headed straight for the elevator. The elevator doors closed and the car lifted. Doubt invaded Lucille's mind, perching itself underneath her flowered hat. She stared at the floor lights on the panel as she wiped the sweat and make-up mix from her face with a Kleenex.

Ding! The car stopped. The doors opened onto an outer office. Several feet in front of her was Miss Kiwi's office. The outer office was empty, except for an office chair, desk, small couch and a wall clock. No pictures. No computer. No file cabinet. A low buzzing sound, almost inaudible, hummed in her ears and filled the air. Lucille stepped awkwardly and lightly a few feet forward. She squinted her eyes, and tried, but couldn't see through the shaded glass door. Curious, she reached, turned the glass door knob and pushed forward. It was empty. Right away, she caught the sweet smell of incense and candles. She couldn't tell exactly which flavor, but it smelled like burnt cinnamon.

"Come!" a voice ordered from a dark corner. Lucille took small baby steps, clutching her purse tightly, she crossed the threshold.

Kiwi spoke. The tone in her voice changed from that of a general to a mother's soothing calm. "Come in. Sit, my child." Kiwi sat, smiling behind a large, polished oak wood desk and gestured towards a small table off to the side. All of the shades were drawn. The only light came in from the outer office and the lighted candles on the table. Even the noise from the elevated trains and the street outside seemed to be shut out. Kiwi smiled. Lucille studied Kiwi and saw that several of her teeth were missing. Lucille tried to relax as she walked over to the table, while perusing the room. Lucille couldn't tell the exact color of the carpet, walls, the ceiling nor the color of her own dress. By the time Lucille sat down, Kiwi had somehow gotten up from behind the desk, closed the door and was seated opposite her. Kiwi's face had lost her smile and her expression turned serious.

"Did you bring the money?" Kiwi asked. Lucille nodded yes and started to open her purse. Kiwi held up an open hand. "Stop! Not until we are finished." Then she leaned forward, questioning in a sing-song, "Child, what troubles you?"

Lucille cleared her throat. "My husband... he... I need him to stop... if he'd only stop..."

Kiwi urged her on. "Stop doing what he is doing?"

Lucille looked puzzled. "Yes, but let me explain what he's doing."

"No need. I already know. I feel the vibe. It is one of shame, guilt and fear. Everyone in your community knows of his counseling. His service is to the community. It is the reason most of the parishioners favor you. He is counseling as we speak."

Lucille turned away with a shameful look towards the window and then at the floor. "What should I do? I just want him to stop. It wouldn't be so bad if I didn't have to see these same people every Sunday. Miss Kiwi, you understand, I don't mean no one no harm. I just want..."

Again, Kiwi's hand went up and Lucille yielded. "There is

nothing you can do.

The universe will right itself on its own. It will be nothing but the hand of God. We are not in control. You must believe in the spirit and follow my instructions to the letter."

"How will I know if he stops?" Lucille was starting to feel dizzy. The room became stifling. It didn't feel like this when she first sat down.

"You will know. Just watch the clock."

"What clock? Miss Kiwi, please!"

"Leave the money on the table."

* * *

Lucille began to perspire even worse than when Detective Heathrow had first come in earlier. He didn't look too pleased with her story about Miss Kiwi.

"So, where can I find this Kiwi person? I want to talk to her if you don't mind."

"To tell you the truth, sir, I don't really know. After I left that afternoon, I could never reach her again. The phone was disconnected every time I tried to call and..."

"Don't worry yourself, ma'am. Tell you what—give me that address again and I'll see if I can shoot over there, just to check her out. You'll have to stay in the lock up while I'm gone."

"You mean in a cell? Oh, Lord!"

"I'll leave word, so that you'll be the only one in there, okay? And I don't do that for everybody. But I'll warn you now, there'll be hell to pay if you're sending me off looking for this chick for nothing."

Lucille only half listened. She kept mumbling. "Oh, Lord... Lord. Lord."

She sat on the mattress, arms folded with a blank look on her face. Her mind had faded into a mist. She felt an overwhelming need to hum a song to herself. The same song her mother used to hum to her when she was a little girl. It always brought her peace. She would sit on the floor and lean on her mother's leg while she sang in a low voice and stroked Lucille's head and combed her thick, black hair. She always teased Lucille that she would take a pair of shears one day and cut it the next time she was bad. The next time never came as far as Lucille was concerned. Her mother took sick and died six months later. From then on, it was as if her father couldn't marry her off fast enough. If she didn't marry, it would break his heart. She would not fulfill her duty as a daughter. He also insisted that she go to church. This was where Hezekiah's touch took hold.

"You know when my granddaddy's gone they'll expect me to pick up where he left off?" Hezekiah spied Lucille from the corner of his eye with an inquiring look.

"Hmm, and you need a wife. What would a brother minister with a big ole congregation like this do without a First Lady? That would be blasphemous, wouldn't it?" Lucille laughed to herself.

"Watch out now, girl. You might have just what I need, but don't get too hainty on me," Hezekiah said. "You ain't the only fish, you know?"

Periodically, a female officer would saunter past. After the fifth time, she stopped. "Funny, you don't look like a murderer."

Lucille felt insulted, snapping back at the officer. "What's a murderer supposed to look like?" The officer had rekindled a boiling pot of intense feelings in Lucille. She reminded her of Eva, the one who broke Lucille's back.

Six months earlier, Eva had begun sitting in the second pew

of the sanctuary-a painted portrait, wearing wigs, lashes and make-up. Eva sat, a mirrored opposite of Lucille on the other side of the church. Eva's dresses had slowly changed their colors and patterns to those of red and pink flowers. The rumor mill started, and as much as Lucille tried to cover her ears and shield her heart, the stinging would not quit. Even the children in the Sunday school classes giggled and pointed. They had heard the whispers of their parents. Once edged on by one of the deacon's wives, Lucille gathered up the nerve to confront Eva.

Eva stood fast, with an all-knowing smile that had clean up woman written all over it. "If you can't keep him happy, what do you expect?"

Lucille gave up and left the building with Willie dragging behind, pretending he didn't know what had just transpired and why. That afternoon Lucille got the call from the deacon's wife, who had seen and heard everything and mentioned Kiwi as a remedy. After all, it had worked for her.

Lucille wondered what time it was. She sat and stared at the corner of the gray, concrete floor. A calm, serene feeling wrapped itself around her. Detective Heathrow had been gone for a while.

It has to be at least three in the morning, she thought.

The deep purple of the night sky had taken over by now. Ms. Kiwi should be able to set him straight and put an end to all this foolishness. Whatever it was that had happened, they couldn't blame her—all she did was follow Kiwi's instructions. A lock of Hezekiah's hair, placed in a crystal shot glass, buried three inches deep into the ground, exactly six feet from the back of the house in the middle of the yard at midnight. Kiwi assured her this would definitely break the spell these evil women had put on him.

"It will never work," Lucille said to herself. "Just a waste of Hezekiah's money spent on Ms. Kiwi."

Then, Lucille heard the commotion down the hall. "Let her out! Just let her out, goddamnit!" Detective Heathrow clamored loudly.

Lucille heard the female officer's protests. "Detective, what happened? She put a spell on you too?"

Lucille sighed and swung her head slightly to the side, while ignoring the noise outside the cell and listening for the rumbling underneath her feet. The water. The river. The ocean. Whatever it was, it was moving. Talking—speaking her language, saying something to her. The next thing she heard was the cell door, sliding and opening. The female officer beckoned Lucille to come forward and pointed. Lucille stood up, smoothed her dress and stepped into the corridor. She could see Heathrow further down the hall.

As she got closer, his face became clearer, but he looked different. A glazed look draped over his eyes. His hair and suit was disheveled. He looked like he wanted to say something but couldn't articulate it at all. Lucille brushed past without speaking.

The taxi pulled up in front of the house. Lucille got out and started towards the walkway and up the steps. She stopped briefly at the door and looked up at the stars that dotted the sky. The driver pulled away. She got up her courage and entered. She made a beeline straight to her easy chair. *HIS & HERS* was knitted on the shawls that covered the backs. She picked up her knitting ball and decided to finish knitting Hezekiah's sweater. Lucille glanced at the clock on the mantle. It said eleven o' clock.

Sonnyman

Adams' barbershop was where we all used to hang. It was also where we heard the news. Sonny was dead. The air went out of me as I sat there in the chair, thinking about when I last saw him two years ago. He had been ill, losing weight, no appetite. He never said exactly what it was. In fact, he was very secretive about the whole thing. Because he was Sonny, I didn't press him about it. I was just glad to see him.

That afternoon, all he wanted to talk about was his music. He had been a bass player for some thirty odd years. Sonny kept saying he needed a break. Some rest from all the traveling.

We were on our third cup of coffee as he segued into a story about being on the road.

"California is not the place to be if you want to keep your head straight," Sonny said, rubbing his eyes. They glowed as he talked about the women, the money, the shooting galleries, the busts and all of the contracts almost signed.

I tried to change the subject. "Why don't you just settle down and teach music? At least you could do private lessons."

Sonny stared into his cup. "I tried that. But, man... it's just not the same as being on stage, y'know?"

The sun in the window looked in on us, but it wasn't very warm outside. Not in Chicago's October. It was the middle of the month and the first real sign of the changing of the seasons was in effect. As Sonny went on about his exploits, I spied several teens on their way home from school. The sight conjured up memories of me, Sonny, CB and Head. Four musketeers, ready to take on the world and everybody in it.

We would make our way home from basketball practice, trying to make it to the bus stop without getting into a fight. The Gaylords, the white gang, were always riding past in their Chevys giving us the finger. We would holler something back about their mothers' lineage and continue to roll up joints.

Sonny brought me back to the present. "Say, man, you still with me? You ain't heard a word I said in the last fifteen minutes, have you?"

"I'm sorry, man. Just got some things on my mind."

"What kind of things be more important than me? We see each other once a year and you can't sit here and carry on a conversation with your old buddy. What's up with you?"

I knew Sonny was just fucking with me. I also knew that he knew that I suspected something was wrong. Very wrong. It was like a last will and testament, only he couldn't bring himself to say it aloud to me. Sonny knew that I would understand when the time was right. The waitress sauntered over to our table again with a smile, hoping we'd order something to eat. We finally obliged.

She brought our steaks and eggs and graciously set the plates on the table. I wandered again while Sonny talked. It seemed like we'd all come out of the womb together, even though we didn't meet until we wound up at the same school in sixth grade. We made it an unsaid competition.

In eighth grade, we all scored pretty high on the Iowa tests and our teacher cared enough to talk to our parents about pushing us out of the neighborhood and into a high school on the northwest side. Everyone knew, however, that it was an all boy's vocational high school though. The signifying we put up with from our friends when we came home at the end of the day was brutal.

"Prosser pussies!" They would say and laugh in our faces as we passed pints of White Port mixed with Kool-Aid. But nobody ever transferred though. We knew deep down they secretly wished they were there too. It helped that we all played basketball and still kept up the grades. That demanded some respect and cooled down some of the harassment. In the summer, we would really get back at them on the court, in the park. Every now and then, our coach would set up a preseason practice scrimmage with Austin High. We lost more than we won. But when we'd win, we'd milk it for all it was worth. Summer in the park was the place to be.

Sonny had finished more than half of his meal. But it looked like he forced down every bite. As if he couldn't swallow.

"Look man, you better eat that shit. I'm paying for it. You remind me of one of my band mates, the skinny one."

Sonny laughed uncomfortably to himself. He looked like the piano player who struggled to hit the next note while you prayed that he would. I looked up from my plate and half smiled. I finally started to see the real Sonny again. The one who would hog the ball as well as the joint. The one who would screw all the girls we considered ugly and nobody else wanted. Back then, we laughed. But Sonny laughed too. I saw the Sonny who never quite made the big time but still managed to eke out a living in music. He knew something we didn't know—what it meant to live while dying. I wondered if he had accepted it or if he was trying to live around it. Sonny never let on. He just wanted to remind me. People lie just because they lie. Sonny hated people

24

who lied.

"You just a big ass liar!" Sonny liked to say to the latest girl he was trying to hustle. He'd always be able to mess up their heads with that line. Make them believe something about themselves that wasn't true. In the end, he'd always get the drawers. Sonny was a true judge of character. Intuitive to the bone. He could spot the bullshit a mile off. I thought I knew Sonny better than any of us. Knew his mother, his brother and his sister. Never got to know his father though. He had left the family when Sonny was only two years old and Sonny always resented the man for it.

Years later, when he ran into Sonny and me on Madison Street, Sonny cursed him out and used his famous lines about liars. Only this time, Sonny was serious, dead serious. And he was hurt, but trying to play it hard. It was amazing, their resemblance. Both five-foot-seven. Close cropped hair cut, wavy and parted on the side. Stylish dressers. Right down to the choice in color of the suits they had on. Sonny always had an eye for the clothes and I never knew where he'd gotten it. I guess it was in the genes. Afterward, I told Sonny that he didn't have to front his old man like that just because I was there. Sonny mumbled to himself, turned and started towards his house. I would see him in the morning as always.

The waitress had made her way back over to our table as I refocused on the present. "Can I get you guys anything else? More coffee?"

"No thanks, baby." Sonny gulped another piece of bread. "But I could use one more thing since you asked."

She bit on it whole. "What's that?"

"You, in a glass."

The waitress's half-smile and raised eyebrow told us that was

25

lame and she'd heard better. "From the looks of you, you're barely keeping in the steak you just scarfed down." She backed up and walked away.

Sonny was drowning, trying to keep pace with the rest of the band. By the sweat on his face, Sonny was hoping they would throw him a life preserver and fast. The notes were like bubbles. They just kept on popping up and every time you hit one, it just disappeared into thin air. Sonny was desperate, a dead man in the water being engulfed by the waves. The drummer kept looking away from him to the left trying to hear where the groove was taking them. Sonny gasped for air with every turn. The drummer and the bass man had to hold the beat and clear the road for everyone else to follow, even if it is a slow blues journey.

"What the matter with you, boy? Can't hang tonight?"

"Oh, I can hang... I can *hang!* See when we get out of here tonight and take that flight back to Chicago, I'll be alright. I'll be alright. I'll be alright..."

Ronnie had sensed that Sonny was floundering and trying to find his way and that the audience was getting restless. Sonny breathed easier with the banter Ronnie had created. The pace picked up and the song, an original composition by Ronnie, was something Sonny was familiar with and liked to play. The tune was melancholy, blue yet soothing and prayerful. Ronnie was a Muslim and embraced the belief wholeheartedly. He didn't play around, so his music was very serious to him.

He would scold Sonny from time to time when he knew Sonny was popping. "How could you destroy your temple like that, man? We only got one. You keep tearing down the bricks and trying to cement 'em back in, chipping away at the foundation. That's why you so shaky, Sonny. That shit gon' make your heart stop one of these days."

Sonny would always be repentant, then defiant. "I'll do better, man. This is the last time. If I had a dollar for all the times y'all said you cared about me... shit, I wouldn't have to work no more." Sonny played pocket pool to cool his embarrassment. "But you know you can't tell a grown man what to do and when to do it. I know what I'm doing, how much to do and where to do it and who to do it with."

Ronnie shook his head. "So that makes it justifiable?"

Sonny shuffled his feet, snorted and wiped his nose. "Man, you just don't understand. It's not like what you think at all. I stopped the needle long time ago. Burn a little membrane here and there, but ain't nothing going under my skin, y'know? I knew cats who couldn't figure out their last names after they did it up. Not me. Not *me*, boy. If I ever lose this heaven, I'll know something ain't right."

Ronnie laughed and shook his head again. "Man, you talking out the side of your neck. Just make sure you make the gig. Got that?"

I sat and looked at Sonny and wondered what it was he wanted me to do exactly. Sonny was worn out, tired and used up. I wondered how he could continue to eat and put on a face that was supposed to cover up the hurt. Sonny was like life in that respect, always trying to cover up the pain. I wondered—what about Eileen? Did she know about his health? Probably, but I didn't want to broach the subject. I waited and tried to feel Sonny out.

Sonny read my eyes. "Eileen? Yeaah, we talked. But y'know how it is. I can still put my finger on her if I have to. She still has my heart. Never let it go, matter of fact. Most of what I played was based on my feelings for her, especially the blues things. She was my girl, but we just couldn't make. Y'know how I used to always play 'em and tell 'em they was full of lies?"

I played with my fork. "Yeah, man, you had that down pat. But you lost your skills over the years."

Sonny's eyes widened. "I can still do 'em up when I want to. But anyway, I never told anyone this, but Eileen was the one I couldn't play. She was too real. Love pierced my head and my heart. I could only see her one way. Beautiful! There was nothing ugly about her. I remember the first time I kissed her. Tasted like carnation baby milk. Ooh shit! More than once had to run home and change my drawers."

I chuckled to myself and tried to cover it up. *Sonny... a romantic? Shiiiiit!*

Sonny continued. "Yeah man, Eileen was the one. She was the one. She knew it when we was 17. She knew it when we was 22 and trying to live together..."

I cut him off. "But you couldn't leave that shit alone, could you? You just had to keep popping. You blew it, man! Admit it."

Sonny grew angry. "Look man, I got no regrets for nothing. I had to do what I had to do. If you played like I played, then you'd know. Wake up in the morning, head busting with all kinds of music. Couldn't keep it in, couldn't let it out. It's like standing on a rooftop and leaning over the edge and soaring up into the clouds. But, man, I ain't apologizing for nothing to nobody. I didn't deserve her and she didn't deserve me. Yeah, I was a sucker sometimes. But she was a sucker too!"

"I hope you had sense enough to tell her to go get tested. All she ever did was try to love you. But you couldn't deal with it, could you? Tell the truth and shame the devil!"

Sonny looked to the other side of the room. His head sort of bobbed and wavered to the side as if he was trying to hear that one note that would bring it all together. If he found it, he would hit it and hit again and again. A life out of sync is nothing funny. He was in suspension, in between talking and thinking. Thinking of a life that was now running out—running on empty. He didn't want to go back to that dangerous place he'd spent so much time trying to get away from and say amen one more time.

Transitions are hard and many can make or break your mind. "Through them, we all seek redemption," Sonny would have said.

CB and Head said that they would chip in. They weren't surprised that he wanted cremation. It was cheaper. There wasn't any religion to attach to him. The music was his religion, all encompassing. Sonny was at his best when he could lose himself in it. It's not that I didn't think Sonny believed. Sonny believed in the Spirit, that's for sure. Otherwise he couldn't have played like he played. His spirit was the source and Sonny tapped into it the only way he knew how. It's just that I knew he didn't go for any other kind of show. I wasn't exactly sure how to approach his mother at the memorial. She never would acknowledge Sonny's problems. He was the apple of her eye and would always be.

Two Hearts

Sitting in this clinic is like sitting in a hole without a floor. No top. No bottom. No walls to touch. No light. Just darkness. I know he said he'd be here an hour ago and he's not here yet. At least I have Reuben to talk to, but Reuben can't talk back. All he can do is open and close his little mouth. Every now and then, he'll wave his little wrinkled hands attached to his short, caramel-colored arms.

Mama hollered at me this morning again, the same way she has been doing ever since Reuben's been around. I don't understand why, because she was cool when she found out Marcello and me was having sex at his house when his Mama wasn't at home. I call him Cello for short. He ain't a bad person—he just leads this charmed life with a charmed smile that appears constantly, 'cause all the girls like him like that. It doesn't help that he's a starter on the basketball team. That's why when he started to talk to me, nobody could believe it. I just stood there in the school cafeteria like a mute, posturing with my feet and hands acting like he didn't mean nothing to me, when all the while, on the inside, my stomach was bubbling and I thought I was gonna throw up all over the floor. Later on that week after an afternoon game, Cello let it be known that we were kicking it. I don't really understand the game as much as he thinks. I just always clap and holler like everybody else when he scores a basket. He's tall and gangly—about six feet, five inches. His skin is a smooth Hershey chocolate. Sometimes, when he's trying to talk and make a point, he gets excited and embarrassed and stutters. I just tell him to take a deep breath and start over again with what he wants to say. He's been in Special Ed classes since we were in third grade. His boys kid him sometimes about being so dark, but he says Michael Jordan is dark-skinned too, so it doesn't make any difference to him. Seems like most people hang around him just because he's so good at playing ball.

Me, I'm light-skinned—high yellow, my granny always says. Then, she laughs. She don't mean no harm, but my mother always cuts her eyes and sucks on her teeth at her when Granny teases me about my complexion.

Mama had me when she was only sixteen. Never married my father, but they still keep in touch. They split up when I was only three, so I don't remember a whole lot about that time. He moved to California and works construction. He sends money when he can. When he heard that I was pregnant with Reuben, he came back to Chicago and stayed for a few days. He came by the house, but didn't say much. He just sat there looking at me every once in a while, chain-smoking Newports and drinking Martel. He and Granny don't get along. She says he ain't got good sense and drinks too much. Then, they got into an argument and she told him to get the hell out and go back to his family in Cali and never come back. She told him Cello looks and smells too much like him.

"Cut from the same cloth," Granny said. He must have been hurt behind that because he hasn't been back since. He's never seen Reuben up close, only the pictures I sent him.

Here comes Nurse Gloria. She's nice. Not like some of the other nurses I've met since I've been coming here. Nurse Gloria even met my mother and told her that she'd take good care of me. She's built like my granny with wide hips and round, sturdy, strong legs. Her graying hair speaks of the same wisdom that Granny has. It's almost like she knew me and Reuben before the first time we came here. Reuben was crying and teething, but when she took him from me, he stopped and fell into a peaceful sleep.

I say she's like Granny, because no matter what happens, she'll stand there with hands on hips and shake her head at me. "You all just don't know, do you?"

Well, what am I 'sposed to know anyway? Granny always speaks like that.

Rueben is awake now. His dark brown eyes dart back and forth from one side to the other. I use my index finger to give him an eye test, just to see if he follows. He does. I wonder if he dreams like me. What would he dream about anyway? I dream a lot since I had him.

I look up at the clock. *Cello, will you come on?* It's two forty-five—still no Cello. He's already one hour and forty minutes late. I rock Reuben and try to think of a song to sing to him, but can't. I look at the walls. Besides the steel blue pamphlet rack leaning against it, there's a fire extinguisher, they're papered with posters about HIV and AIDS and mononucleosis and shaken baby syndrome and SIDS and birth rates and mortality rates and heart disease and everything else that I need to know. How can anybody remember all of that? It's too much! It's enough trying to remember the work I get for homeschooling that ends in a couple of months. I have to go back to graduate on time. I was planning on going to college right after I graduate, but now I don't know. Cello says he got a scholarship, but I ain't seen no paperwork—no letters or nothing. Every time I bring it up, he kind of goes into his shell and says he's got a headache and needs to go. My granny just might be right about him, but I hope not.

Like I say, he's pretty much a nice guy. I don't think his teachers or his family understand him like I do. He'll come by sometimes and we'll sit on the porch, playing with Reuben and watching the cars speed past. He thinks he might not be a good Daddy, 'cause he never knew his own daddy. He don't know if he's dead or alive. He says his Mama never mentions him and nobody else in his family does either. I tell him that I don't really know my own daddy that well; I mean, I know who he is, but I just really don't know him. I just know he sends some money every now and then, but it ain't much cause me and Mama and Granny still struggling like everybody else around here.

One night, Cello got deep on me and started crying and said that he wanted to know his daddy—really wanted to know him. What was he like? Did he look like him? Did he crave chocolate cake like him? Did he stutter like him? Cello favors his mom in color, but not in height. He thinks that maybe his father was tall like him and played ball too. He was wondering if he was special education too. What got me was when Cello said that maybe that's why he don't take to responsibility like he should. He said he knows that sometimes when he's with his boys, hanging out and doing nothing, he knows he should be with me and Reuben. I nodded my head in agreement but felt sad for him at the same time. Seems like he can't do no better than he does, no matter how hard he tries sometimes. I rubbed and stroked his forehead like Granny does mine when I'm depressed. But it does seem like he's never there when I need him. Like the time I came running

33

into the clinic one morning, moaning and crying like Reuben.

Nurse Gloria asked, "What's wrong?"

I said, "Every time I feed Reuben, he throws up all over himself. I mean, I know babies do that, but..."

Then, she cut me off. "Baby girl, little ones like him do that, especially when you feed them too much. Their stomachs are only so big. They can't take a lot of food like us. There's no place else for it to go except right back up. Here, let me take him and clean him up—be right back, okay?"

Nurse Gloria must have a hundred kids—she always knows what to do. Nowadays, I follow the recommended serving amount on the package and try not to feed him every time he cries. Nurse Gloria said it'll only spoil him if I do. It's going on two o'clock and the afternoon appointments start rolling in.

Here comes Sabrina—one in her stroller, one in the oven. I don't know how she does it. I can hardly handle one. We say hello and she takes a seat. We know each other from way back in grammar school. Graduated eighth grade together. Sabrina's cool, but I never really hung around her after graduation. When we were freshmen in high school, she hooked up with some girls who were trouble makers and well known around the school for starting shit with any and everybody. Then the second year started and she left when she got pregnant and hadn't been back. I heard that she went to the pregnant school for girls for a while, but got kicked out for smoking weed. I wonder what she does all day. Never heard that she works at all. Mama knows her mama, but she don't talk too much about her, except to downgrade her. Mama used to always say that if I ever took after Sabrina, she'd break my neck. Link card and all. Well, now I got my baby and the link.

Cello, will you come on? Her son is three and hyper. Granny would say he's got ants in his pants. I watch her and him out of the corner of my eye, trying not to be obvious. Every time she calms him down, she just stares off to the side towards the entry door, cursing to herself and focusing on the black and white floor patterns with a far off, pained look on her face. Granny always says if you want to see how somebody looks for real, look at them while they're in pain. That's when you see the real person. I hope Reuben ain't hyper like that. Late at night, when he's asleep, I just stand there by his crib and look at him, wondering what he'll be like when he's older. Maybe he'll be a teacher. A doctor? A lawyer? President? I don't know.

If Reuben could talk, I wonder what he'd say. I've wondered that ever since the day the doctor handled him from me amidst all the blood and shit. Did he say goodbye to God just before he came into the world? Did the lights above bother him? How does he see me when he looks at me? Does he see the same thing that my Mama sees? I started asking my Mama these questions days after we came home and she just looked dumbfounded, like I was crazy.

A couple days later, I overheard Mama on the phone talking to Aunt Joanie about how she was really worried about me and might make me go see a doctor if I kept on talking and asking stupid questions about Reuben. I just threw it out of my head, went back into my room and sat on my bed. I sat there and watched Reuben. He laid there and I think he was smiling. He was trying to reach out or grab at something I couldn't see. His eyes looked beyond me and at something else. He was just having a good time. Granny says that when babies did that, they were playing with the angels that hovered just above them.

Cello, will you come on?

Every time I'd screw up and feel like the world is doing me

wrong, Granny would try to comfort me. "Honey, God gave us two hearts. One to put out there to the world, 'cause it's gonna get broke. The other one? Well, that's yours for safe keeping." Then she'd rub my forehead with soft hands and keep braiding my hair in a circle. She says it's so everything will always come back to me.

Popped (Observations On A Bus Ride Home)

The moment the taxi driver pulled into the bus station, I knew something was up. I had forgotten this was still a rural town, even though it's in Illinois' state capital where the governor resides, it was closed from twelve to two, Monday through Friday.

"Ain't that 'bout nothing," I mumbled to myself, struggling to get my bag out of the back seat. The driver was nice enough to help me take the other bags out of the trunk. Two young people waited outside by the station's entrance. It was a windy, unusually chilly autumn Friday afternoon. I surmised that they either were runaways or burned out hypes, waiting to rob me of what little money I had after the cab driver left. As the driver pulled away, he waved his hand thanking me for the tip. They looked me over without being too obvious. I think they figured I might be carrying because of the way I tried to look streetwise back at them.

The first question came from the young man standing. "Got an extra cigarette on you?" He looked so sincere. I laughed inwardly to myself and tried to hide my grin.

I half-smiled and responded stoically. "Nah man." I tried to give the impression I was from the city and a *'don't mess with me'* shrug.

"Damn," he said under his breath as he spun and returned to his spot on the cold ground. The young girl, sitting against the wall with her knees pulled up to her chest, laughed to herself and hunched her shoulders to fight back the cold. She was white and looked about sixteen. Our breaths were frosted by the high wind. The station sat adjacent to some kind of factory warehouse. Several compact cars were parked against its wall and the building rested against a backdrop of tree branches that had already shed their leaves, reaching upwards into the sky like thin, gray-brown fingers. I took a seat on the edge of one of the two white flower pots, used as ashtrays that stood guard on each side of the entrance, hoping it might take my mind off the wait while my watch stared back at me.

The young girl could hold out no longer. I think she wanted to let me know that she was not with the young man sitting next to her. She wanted to make it known that she was from the South-side of Chicago—one of the projects maybe. Her inflections and expressions were full of hood slang and black dialect. Clearly, she had been raised around black folks. Underneath her blond hair, a road map of red pimples ran up and down her milky white skin. I thought it interesting that she was trying so hard to let me know that she could talk the talk. Every now and then, I would nod approval and smile when she made remarks about how badly life had treated her and her "peeps."

Her cell phone rang and she looked at it with disgust. "Man, why they keep blowing me up? I told 'em I wouldn't be there until late. They probably want to know if I got any weed with me. I can't do nothing anyway, 'cause I'm pregnant!" She pushed the phone back into pocket and kept rambling on to herself.

I had assumed that she just had a potbelly and wore jeans

that were too tight. "I used to stay on 47th. But I just had too much trouble with some of those females over there—know what I'm saying? So my case worker said she was going to place me somewhere where I could stay out of trouble. Someplace I could finish high school without getting shot."

"Finish high school?" I said to her, feigning interest. "You look..."

"I know. That's what everybody say. But I'm 21 last week. I just look young." She giggled to herself—her own little secret joke on the world. I still thought she was lying.

The young man spoke again. "Man, can I use your cell phone?"

"Depends on where you're calling."

"Aw, man. It's here in Springfield! I just want to call my girl and tell her to come on and get me. I'm tired of waiting for this stupid ass bus, know what I'm saying?"

At first, I hesitated. "Yeah, here." I handed him the phone, trying to give a look that said if you call long distance, I'll shoot you. The young girl sat, smiling at us. I think she was trying to see if old boy would try to make that long distance call, but he didn't.

He played it perfectly. "Baby? Where I'm at? I'm tired of waiting on this bus! You comin'? Well, com'on! Awright! See you when you get here! What? I told you they stuck me up—took everything I had. If my boy didn't loan me this money, I'd still be there. What? Yeah, I got to pay him back! Just com'on, okay?"

He gave my phone back and thanked me. I made a point of taking the phone from him, while still conversing with the young girl, just to try and look cool. Then, he started into a long rambling story about how he had been in Las Vegas for a fight and how he got jumped and robbed. I sat and listened, nodding.

All had become a quiet wait. I put on my headphones, turned

on the radio and listened to the local rock station. Every now and then, I or the young girl would look towards the entrance to the lot and let out an exaggerated sigh, knowing that we still had at least an hour to go before the station's teller would return.

A few minutes later, a compact Honda pulled into the lot. The young man's magic had worked. His girl sped over, maneuvered a three point turn and stopped. The young man grabbed his bags and jumped into the car. They sped off in a hurry. Spying his girl's face through the windshield, she looked bothered. I wondered whether she was really where she wanted to be and happy to see him. As they drove off, he was already running his mouth, probably about his latest Las Vegas experience.

By now, he young girl had made herself a semi-pallet with her luggage. She lay partially sideways. She closed her eyes and pretended to sleep, but I knew she was watching me. Time passed, no teller. A Cook County Sheriff's van pulled up into a space a few steps away. I took off the headphones and sat as straight as I could without toppling over. The guard got out and a young man followed. He was dressed in a thin, navy blue sweat suit and flat, nondescript gym shoes of the same hue. His braids ran diagonally, up and down the side and top of his head. He had the demeanor and movement of a panther who had just been let out of a cage and ready to strike. He kicked his legs out, backwards and forward, like a runner at the starting line. The deputy said some words to him that I couldn't hear. The passenger nodded affirmatively, while holding a small plastic bag. He walked briskly towards us as the deputy drove away. We both politely said hello and let him in on the reason why we were sitting outside in the cold. He didn't waste any time asking for and being told we didn't have any cigarettes. He and the young girl seemed to hit it off. They reminisced about Chicago.

"The corrections academy?" The young girl knew all along.

"You know it!" He stamped his feet and folded his arms across his chest trying to generate some heat. "Man, is it a store around here?"

"Yeah. See those stop lights way down there?" She pointed northward and laughed.

"Damn!" He ended his cigarette search and started into his history. Man, I'm so glad to get out of there. Cause I can't go back—know what I'm saying? Got a lil' shorty I ain't even seen."

She was excited now. "You ain't seen him yet?"

"Naw. His Mama wouldn't bring him down. Talking 'bout her Mama say a boy ain't 'sposed to see his daddy like that. Don't matter if he's only two months old."

"So you never seen him?"

"I seen some pictures. But you know that ain't like..." His voice trailed off into sadness only he knew.

"How long you been in?" The young girl quizzed further.

"Six months. My girl was five months when I got popped. I was just trying to look out for my guy. Po-Po rolled up on us and he ran—we wasn't doing nothing. I knew I was dirty anyway. So I just told myself *fuck it.* I knew the judge was gon' jam me up—I'll go'n do this short time. But it's the last time. I got a lil' shorty and, man, I got to take care of him."

"Yeah, yeah." The young girl nodded her head.

Time passed and another van rolled in. I realized we weren't very far from a minimum security corrections facility. These guys didn't look hardcore, but they had committed crimes and served out their sentences. This time when the deputy emerged, he opened the door and three others alighted from the back. All three had on the thin gym suits and shoes. As soon as they hit the air, they were freezing too.

Two of the men looked fairly young. The third one, however, looked to be in his late forties or perhaps his early fifties. I took a chance and looked him straight in the eyes. He lowered his head slightly as if he were embarrassed that we were close to the same age. Maybe he was older than me—I don't know. He was five-foot-five with white streaks in his hair and a muscular build like a boxer who had trained in the gym for years. He looked familiar though, like someone I'd known in my past, someone I might have sat next to in grammar school, someone who was probably the smartest kid in the class—certainly not a convict. His afro was 70s era and neatly lined. Someone in the joint must have done him a favor.

He finally nodded at me silently, as if to say "You know the play. Yeah, I'm as old as you think I am. For some reason, I just never got it together." My mind started to turn back the pages, backtracking to the 60s and 70s. I thought about my own life and that, but for the grace of God, thirty years ago and thirty seconds in the wrong direction, I could have been him.

I was brought back to the present by the exchange between the two young men standing in front of me. They had found some common ground. "Man, you knew him?"

"Yep. Man, ole boy was y'know... man! They popped him five times! Five times! I was like... why they do him like that?! Man, I was just with him that night. I left him on the spot. He said he was gon' hold it down. But when I got back to the crib, my sister was standing in the doorway—told me she had just heard about it. She was trying to keep my moms calmed down, 'cause they thought that I was with him. We had rolled out together earlier that morning, trying to make some ends, y'know?"

"Man, I didn't know him like that. But, y'know, we was cool, y'know?"

"Yeah..." The young man looked downward and shuffled his feet on the walkway.

* * *

The ticket teller pulled up in his dark blue economy car. I looked at him as he stepped from his car, discarding a cigarette. The wind chased him as he hustled towards us to unlock the door. He was a short and thin Middle Easterner with a black, bushy mustache and receding hairline. A gigantic sigh of relief came from us all at once, and as soon as he opened the door, everyone politely barged in and lined up at the counter. I decided to sit. Rubbing my hands together, I rested and took in the warmth of the lobby. I rested my legs and listened to the men complain about how much money had been deducted from their commissary to pay for tickets. I stared at the candy machines, carefully weighing which kind of junk food I would buy before getting on the bus. Like most everyone else, as I got my tickets, I bought cigarettes. He didn't have my brand, but when you're having a fit, you don't argue.

Several minutes later, deputies rode up in another van. All three got out and came into the lobby. One of the deputies took a head count and sent a silent message to the brothers who stood around that when he and the other deputies came back later, they had better be on that bus heading to Chicago. The young men respectfully held their banter from low to mid-volume. Another van came and dropped off about fifteen new passengers. This group was different though, a few whites, blacks and Hispanics. So much for diversity. One of the deputies bought the tickets. Then, he passed out the tickets according to a list he held in his hands.

Periodically, some impatient soul would step outside and brave the high winds to smoke. Even the ticket teller left his post and took a break. When he came back in, the phone rang. The look on his face and the nodding of his small head told me something was wrong. His pronouncement a moment later brought about a series of groans, grumbling and low-level cursing. The approaching bus was already thirty minutes late. Even worse, it was nearly full. Then, he announced there was another dispatched bus running twenty minutes behind it from St. Louis and there would be more than enough room. I waited until everyone else ran up to the counter and had badgered him to repeat the same information he had just given before I went. His advice to me was to wait for the second bus.

He was right. When the first bus pulled in, there were only six or seven seats open. Several of the men jockeyed for position on the side of the bus under the watchful eye of the sheriffs. The bus driver came into the lobby looking worn and tired, like he couldn't wait to get to Chicago. He held a brief conversation with the teller, then left. He sped off with as fast as that coach could roll down the street towards the highway.

I took another seat and surveyed the room. The noise had become more tolerable than before. Even though it was still early, the sun was starting to take its seat behind the clouds. I sat and listened to the inmates again. The white one, with the long brown hair and deep set Jim Morrison eyes would not stay still.

He spoke loudly to one of his buddies. "Man, I sure hope my uncle ain't home when I get back. He'll only get me in trouble." He wiped his brow and nose several times. He gave me the impression that he was *really* hoping that his uncle would be there.

The lady from St. Louis who had disembarked from the first bus declared her independence in answer to a question from one of the men who hailed from the same place. "Ain't nothing there for me no more. I ain't never going back. Never!" She shifted her leg crossing while making her point.

The brother remained inquisitive. "Damn, baby, what happened? Can't be that bad. You know that's where I'm from? Okay, what street you grow up on?"

"Fifth and State. So, you know what was over there!"

"Yeah, I been there. Did you know Lil'Man and his family?"

"I knew Lil' Man, but I didn't know the family. It was enough knowing him. That nigger was *crazy*!"

The brother intoned in agreement. "Man, they ran that whole set! I knew all of 'em. But they helped keep those other niggers off my ass, y'know? I used to run with all of 'em before I got popped."

Tired of his questions, she ended the conversation. "Yeah, I know what they did—and they did some rank stuff. Like I say, I didn't know nobody but Lil' Man."

The second bus made its turn into the lot and everyone moved towards the door. I was ready to go. I realized that the ride would be a little more than interesting. The driver was a woman. I must admit that I was somewhat surprised that her company would allow her to drive what with all of these men. She definitely had my respect. The guys were all on the bus by now. Most headed for the back. There were so many empty seats that one could sleep comfortably for a few miles. I wavered back and forth for a while, finally deciding that if I didn't at least nap every now and then, the others might think it strange.

About halfway home, we pulled up to a rest stop. McDonalds sure looked good. I stepped down off of the bus and into the wind. It had died down somewhat from its wildness earlier in the morning. I lit a cigarette while stretching and shuffling my feet in the dirt before going into the restaurant. Through the smoke, I stared forward into the forest preserve and let my mind relax. Autumn waved its invisible hands and moved the leafy, downstate backdrop of orange and green from side to side like a slow-motion film.

The driver came in after me and stood in line. I invited her to cut in front of me and place her order. "Got to keep you happy, y'know?" We took seats at separate tables directly across from each other. The French fries were hot and tasty and I was hungry. "You been driving long?"

She smiled. Rolling eyes told me that she'd fielded that question a hundred times before. "Too long. I know some of those guys. A few of them have rode with me several times. I always tell them that I don't want you riding my bus no more—not like this. They always promise me that they won't, but they always do. I 'spose it's all good though. They've never bothered me or nothing like that. Fact, some of the old timers wouldn't allow it anyway. Just like old boy sitting behind you." She nodded towards the guy whose hair looked like mine. "He ain't a bad guy—he just can't stay clean. Like I say, though... let one of them young bucks in the back get too rowdy, he'll set 'em straight."

* * *

Chicago was only about fifty miles away. I tried to nap, but couldn't hit that note. Too much noise. The closer we got to the city, the more hyper the young men in the back became. Their words became pleas of anonymous prayers, one after another.

"Man, I hope my girl be there. I ain't got no bus fare!"

"Man, please! My girl *better* be there! She know she don't want me to have to go off like that. But, y'know she was the only one who had my back when I got popped, know what I'm saying? Man, if your girl ain't there—where you stay? We'll drop you off, okay?"

"Man, y'all ain't got to do that. Somebody'll be there."

"No, man, it's cold out there. You can't be rolling like that. We stuck together in the joint, we stick together out here."

Finally, we moved onto the exit ramp and onto the city streets. A memory jogged. A finger pointed. "Man, I was right there when I got popped. Damn! They took that building down already? Ain't been but a year."

The older brother had had enough. "Look, man, y'all chill okay? I been sitting here listening to y'all the last hundred miles and all I hear is *Man, when I get back... man, when I got popped... man, old girl this... man, old girl that...*" He flailed his arms with exaggerated motions for emphasis. "Man, y'all better recognize! This life ain't a joke. I been out here thirty years chasing that thang and still ain't got it right. Don't y'all know people get tired of coming to pick you up? I'm lucky my sister coming to get me now. But she already told me this is the last time! I'm telling you, your people will eventually get tired of your mess, even your own mama! But, this is *my* last time—you can believe that, young bloods! Y'all young. Don't be stupid all of your lives like me!"

The silence was more than deafening. It was walking up and down through the aisle like a priest throwing holy water on the congregation, blessing and touching everyone riding. Nervous movement in the back wasn't a sign of disrespect. It was a sign of recognition. I turned and looked up at him as he had risen from his seat. The fire in his eyes burned through us all. For a second, I thought he'd launch into a sermon. But, he stopped and lowered his head. The fire had turned to doubt—his face, almost apologetic.

We pulled onto Harrison Street and into the downtown station. Everyone broke for the door. I said my goodbyes to the driver. She shook her head from side to side and smiled. Another ride home. She was headed back to St. Louis to see her daughter. Before she left, she told me she might look into another line of work. The money was good, but it was starting to get to her. I grabbed my bags and limped towards the front of the station, hoping that someone would be there to pick me up.

JT's Song

the blues hand of the Mississippi healer
    told me to call Esu, the witch doctor
    mr. Lucky done gone and left me
no longer standing at the side of my bed
gone on down the road!
the whipping post and devil
wait for me at the end of the line
like a fool I done sold my soul!
the knife stroke was pure and clean...
from "Mississippi Murder"

JT opened the door and his cigar fumes and the scent of motor oil walked in before he did. JT's short stature and bow-legged stance mirrored an old school running back who had endured one too many hits, cuts and bruises, but still kept moving forward. The activity paused, as it usually did when he entered. A long time ago, his reputation on Chicago's west side as a blues musician preceded him. Even though he only nodded towards the older men in the shop, the younger customers gave a quick, respectful glance and always knew there was something different about him. Cordial greetings and a soul embrace was exchanged between JT and the shop's owner: his best friend,

Mr. B. A smile appeared and the worried look left B's face when JT gave him the good news about his car. It would live and run for the rest of the summer at least.

"So what's goin' on?" JT spoke, smiled, showing his pink gums. Oil and dirt were lodged between his nails and fingers. He was indeed a working man.

"Nothing, man. Nothing. Ain't nothing new under the sun." B moistened his lips and circled them with his tongue before it rested on the side of his mouth. He sized up how to continue the cut of the young man's head. Young people these days were so damn particular about the littlest things.

JT always had to have the last word whenever they talked. "Depends on which sun you looking at. Some suns are brighter than others. But we all need at least one."

A hot sun had already reached down and snatched up what was left of a humid, but cool overnight sleep. It beamed down against the plate glass window facing Madison Street and its people. On the other side stood a snapshot, the lifeblood and main vein of the Westside. The scene spoke and sang the sensibilities of a people. The people who had migrated from Mississippi, Alabama and other places south some fifty years earlier—searching, praying and hoping for a better life. People buzzed back and forth like bees looking for a hive of refuge. The children ran into the rib joints, McDonalds and Popeyes with empty stomachs and out with bags of food in hand. Street merchants strolled up and down the walk, carrying and selling their items for discounted prices. Others offered their wares from the side doors of their vans and cars, while the crackheads, the prostitutes, the liars, the thieves and anyone else who would try to get in where they could fit in, all became a part of the mix. JT and B had witnessed the good and the bad of the street over the last forty years. B had moved his shop several times over, but somehow he always managed to find a store front to settle into and stay long enough for his clientele to find him and return. They were always faithful. Even his original customers' grandchildren came to B to get their hair cut.

"When you goin' back down home? You comin' with me next month, or are you gonna stay away like you always do?" B goaded and taunted JT like a strawberry cake sitting on the table in front of a fat man on Thanksgiving. You know I want you, but I don't need you.

JT looked away, wiped his brow with his handkerchief and blew his nose while he measured his words. "B, why you always bringing up the past?"

He looked down on JT like a father who had caught his son in a lie. "Man, the past don't never leave. It just hides from us. Every now and then, it'll peek around the corner and laugh at us, just to let us know it's still there. Who do you think you're fooling?"

JT pretended to ignore him and laid his hankie out over his thigh. The oil-soiled blue mechanic's uniform showed itself through the cloth. JT folded it with the same precision he'd done for the past fifty years—corner to corner to form a triangle, fold in half and then again before placing it in his shirt pocket.

B continued to rag on him. "The past, huh? You been running so long, the past might've forgotten you."

The remark finally hit home. JT raised his stubbed hand to his neck and gently rubbed the fifty-year old scar. B might as well have swiped a butcher knife across the very place JT massaged. He stared through the window and watched the moving pictures meld into a darkened country road.

* * *

"Com'on, JT. We gon' be late, brother! Mr. Wells's gon' pitch one for sure when he see us." Simon scurried down the dust road, a few steps ahead of JT. The tall red oaks shadowed the willows and held an endless corridor on each side of the road. JT looked up and thought that these trees must be as ancient and old as man. It was a clear night and green leaves stood out and waved down at them from its deep, dark blue background, accented by a sprinkling of silver stars. JT thought the trees had eyesnand had seen it all—the slave ships, the burnings, the hangings, the Civil War, the emancipations—if they knew nothing else, they knew the truth. Simon playfully balanced his guitar on his left shoulder. JT held his guitar securely under his arm. He thought it safer. There was no way he was going to drop his beloved guitar. It had cost him two weeks' pay and then some.

Straight ahead up the road, they could see the lantern lights hanging from the short trees. The guiding light of the lanterns weren't needed tonight. The sky was clear and the moon's beam cast an ominous, mysterious light on JT and made him uneasy. The triangle shaped top and wooden, slanted roof sides leaned slightly to the right. At its foundation, its four corners sat on bricks of different heights. It had been a shotgun, modified to hold a bar, a low platform for the band, several tables and chairs and a small dance floor space. As JT and Simon got closer, they heard the joyous shouts, the good-natured cursing and the night reverie of a boss party. They slowed their hurriedness to a confident strut.

"Com'on, JT," Simon quickened his steps again. "They probably passing the jug by now and messing around with yo' slow ass, I'll miss it!"

"You know I don't mess with that stuff. You shouldn't either. Ain't gon'do nothing but make you wake up with a bad head! And you know your wifey ain't gon' go for that!"

Before going up the steps, they fixed their clothes, tucking in shirts, straightening ties and brushing hair. They rushed up the stairs and swung open the door. The body heat of the patrons inside blew out with a force and stopped them in their tracks. The cool night air that snuck in with them was a welcome relief. The band sat fixed in shirts and ties. Everyone was required to wear his Sunday's best when performing. Since they were relatively new, Mr. Wells rode JT and Simon like a drill sergeant. Every now and then, a veteran player would show with missing ties, slightly drunk or without matching colors just to get on Wells' nerves. No one would be surprised when it resulted in a fist fight between Wells and those who defied him. The musicians on the stage waved and motioned for JT and Simon to hurry and get set up.

Wells admonished them for being tardy. "So, I guess you boys wanna get paid for a whole night, huh? Well, you got another thing coming." Wells drew on his half-smoked cigar and spit on the floor.

JT offered his hand to try and smooth things over. "Mr. Wells, you know we was coming from work. Couldn't get off no earlier."

Wells understood but brushed JT's excuse aside with a disgusted look. "Half work, half pay. We done already played one set. Get ready to sit in on the next one."

* * *

"Say, man. Say, man? You still among the living?" B was

53

standing over JT looking concerned.

"Huh? What?" JT rubbed his eyes and straightened up in his chair. He mimicked a yawn and pretended that he was just waking up.

"I've known you too long, JT. I know what you was doing, same thing you always do when you get spooked about going back. You can't fool me." He smiled, lit a smoke, offered it to JT and lit another one for himself. They commiserated in the moment like two mischievous kids planning the rest of the day. Then, one of B's customers walked in, nodded and headed for the chair. B looked at JT—JT looked up at him. B straightened his neck, wriggled his lean, thin shoulders, put the cigarette out in the tray and left JT and his thoughts to make more money. JT got up, stretched his tired, overworked body and stepped outside onto the street. He took off his glasses, reached for his handkerchief and wiped his brow. He looked right, then eastward towards the sun and squinted from its glare. It had gotten even warmer in just an hour's time. A few doors down in front of the Arab owned grocery store, two men, one younger, one older had stumbled out. A few of the other customers jammed the doorway, urging them on while they argued. JT drew a breath, shook his head in disgust and adjusted his glasses. The younger man in the sky blue frock brandished an open box cutter, threatening the older man. His temples bulged with anger and looked to explode any minute. The older man swaying back and forth was oiled up and full of play. Like JT's, his clothes were dirty, but not because he had been working.

"Man, long as you live, don't you ever put your hands on me!" the young man shouted. "Understand me?" He swung wildly at the man, but missed. The store's owner had come out. He danced gingerly, shadowing the young man's movements, while keeping a safe distance. He cautiously held up his hands in surrender, pleading with him in half-English, half-Arabic. Two other employees had come out and joined the appeal, hoping he'd show some restraint.

The old man continued mock in a loud voice as spit sprayed from his toothless mouth. "Young blood, who you talking to? Huh? Huh? Who you talking to?"

It would be a tragedy, JT thought, if they let him cut that man. The scorching orange-red sun beamed down and didn't help the situation. The water in the pot had boiled over and spilled out into the urban street scene.

* * *

The band played and the lady singer unwrapped her heart with a slow blues. "Baby! You know I love you like I love myself. Baby, if I hurt you, you know I hurt myself..." The crowd blanketed the floor, bumping and grinding to her love call. JT was about to work his solo when a commotion at the bar stopped everything. B and another man had gotten into it. B held his razor high in the air, making ready to swoop down with precision. JT didn't know the intended victim. The lantern strung low from the ceiling and flickered its light against the blade. JT knew that the blade was anything but dull, because B always kept it sharp enough to split a blade of grass.

He spouted whiskey along with his words. "Nigger, the next time I catch you..."

B was caught off guard. He thought the man would just back up and go out of the door once he saw the blade. "Man, I'm gon' give you one last chance. Then, I'm gon' cut you!"

Somehow, the man had gotten his hand on an empty bottle

laying on the bar and flung it into B's face. It caught him flush. B went down and the knife fell from his hand. The unknown offender saw his chance and pounced on B like a starving tiger catching its prey. The band had long stopped playing and joined the crowd, cheering on the man who had the upper hand. JT maneuvered through the crowd and grabbed the assailant by the back of his shirt and pulled hard. Blindly, the man reached down into the saw dusted floor and grabbed B's blade. Then, swiped to the right, then to the left and back and forth. JT tried to hold the man's wrist, twisting it until it broke. Then, JT felt his open flesh hanging from his neck. The red sea parted and ran down his forearm. JT felt the warm liquid, smelled the red scent. The man lay crumpled in pool of red-stained saw dust. The crowd headed for the door in a rush.

The rattling noise of the train's boxcar brought JT back to life. B's face would come into focus and fade out again. JT's face and neck burned like a furnace. He tried reaching up to check it out, but B grabbed his hand and gently lowered it. He tried to talk, but it hurt too much. He closed his eyelids and faded into his dreams. When he woke up again, he was in Chicago, in B's sister's apartment lying on the sofa.

* * *

JT ignored the young man's spitfire stance and grabbed his wrist. Their eyes met. They stared and stared at each other. Neither would flinch until the young man spoke and turned his rage onto JT.

"Man, look, you better let go of me if you know what's good for you."

"It ain't worth it young blood—it ain't worth it."

"Who is you and why you all up in my business? Let me take care of my own—understand me? Now, let me go. This nigger is through!"

"Young blood, if you go through life without killing somebody, you know what?"

"What, man? What?" The young man sweaty face told JT that he had reached his breaking point.

"Then, you doing good," JT said in a low, pleading voice.

By now, the crowd was let down, yet surprised when the young man let JT lower his arm. He closed the blade and put it back in his pocket. The old drunk was sober enough to understand that he had gotten a pass, and took advantage by splitting down the street. Curiosity had gotten the best of B. He and his customers had come out to see what had gone down. They milled about until the excitement blew away with the summer's breeze.

Little Rogue

J eremy awoke. The dream shook him again. He grabbed the car rail and held on for the recoil. The homeless drunk on the other end of the car grumbled, farted, wiped his nose and went back to sleep. He was used to it. Jeremy reached into his right pocket and felt for the box cutter. It was still there.

"End of the line. Everyone must exit the train. "The words rattled around Jeremy's head like pool balls looking for a pocket. He glanced out of the window and saw the motorman's figure reflected in the sunrise backdrop. Jeremy looked at his watch. It said quarter to six. He raised himself from the seat and stretched just as the motorman stuck his head in the door. He looked at Jeremy and flicked his head backwards and to the side. He didn't have to do it twice. The motorman stepped into the car and walked towards the drunk.

"End of the line, baby. Don't care where you go, but you can't stay here." The motorman gave a nudge with his knee.

"Aw, man. Uh, huh." The drunk leaned forward and lurched up to a staggered, half bent position.

"Damn," the motorman covered his nose and mouth. The stench lingered. He followed the dunk, praying for open air at the door.

Jeremy had made his way down the platform and into the

other train, waiting to pull out of the station. He watched the passengers crowd on and jockey for seats. iPads, cell phones, book bags and purses jockeyed too. Jeremy watched, waiting intently for a mark. He couldn't do anything until several stops towards downtown had passed. Like clockwork, he would meet up with Rufus by Central Park. By that time, the train would be good and crowded. Jeremy leaned back, placed his arms around his book bag and pretended to sleep. He could hear the whisper of cymbals bleeding through the headphones of the woman who sat next to him. He thought she was careless. She held her iPhone in front of her for everyone to see. *Here, take me!* Jeremy laughed to himself.

He and Rufus didn't mess with that. The plainclothes were always on the lookout for people snatching those. Besides, the goddamn things might lock up and turn the GPS on automatically. He had recently dismissed two other boys from the group, because they had a hard-on for iPhones. Those marks were easy prey, but attracted too much attention. So now, it was just him and Rufus. Rufus was cool. They had been together since second grade.

Jeremy tried not to, but his thoughts shifted. He tried and tried. He had been trying for the last three days. But, the images kept returning. The flowers. The make-up. The silver lining. The pulpit. The noise they called singing. The plastic smiles of the ushers. The hole in the ground. All of it kept coming back with a vengeance. He saw the last time he sat in Aunt Luella's living room, choking back tears. Listening to the grownups talking about him like he wasn't there. Nobody had asked him anything. He knew one thing though: he wasn't going to stay with that bitch Aunt Luella, even if that's what the court lady said.

Jeremy remembered the last thing his mother had told him.

Everyone had left the room, leaving him and Sylvia for last words. She could barely speak. He had to lean in close to hear her whispered, raspy voice.

"Jeremy, boo?" She always called him that when she really wanted him to listen to her.

"Yeah, Mama. I'm here." His face opened up and his tears baptized him.

"I know...I know," Sylvia managed.

"Yeah, Mama..." He buried his head in the sheets.

"I know I had you and all. But, you know...with everything. With all that happened. I had you. Now, I guess... I got to give you back. Forgive me?"

"I forgive you, Mama."

Sylvia's head slumped over to the side. The beeps turned into one long buzz. The nurses rushed into the room. Someone was pulling Jeremy through the door frame.

"Mama. Mama!" By then, Aunt Luella had him at her breast, stroking his head. He saw the door close behind the doctor who had come to call the time.

"Central Park!" The loud speaker brought him back to the present. More people rushed into the already crowded car. Rufus got on.He and Jeremy made eye contact and smiled. Jeremy got up. He was polite and said excuse me to the lady lost in her music. They both saw the same mark. He had gotten on several stops earlier at Oak Park. Jeremy had been watching him all along. Rufus instinctively knew and elbowed his way next to the man. Just as the train lunged to the next stop, Rufus fell into the mark, grabbing onto his shoulder, faking a fall. Jeremy timed his reach and lifted the wallet and was out the door. Rufus followed suit. They walked briskly down the platform towards the exit doors. Jeremy knew that the mark probably wouldn't know anything until the train pulled into the downtown area round Canal Street.

McDonald's breakfast was especially good that morning. Neither had eaten in two days. The sixty bucks score gave them something to look forward to for the next few days. They had discarded everything else, credit cards, debit cards, pictures and the license.

They walked back to Jeremy's favorite spot. He and Sylvia would meet there when they could. Jeremy sipped his coffee. He looked around and thought he saw Sylvia through the window across the street on Madison. Many times she stood there with the others in front of the Marquis Room, waiting for customers. *The customers would be no more,* he thought. Sylvia's crimes and punishments had been forgiven. He looked at Rufus and understood. Forgiveness was all that the people across the street could ever own.

"Thank God for redemption," he had heard the pastor say at the service.

Jeremy sat on the ground. Only his butt was cold. He cherished the jacket with the fur lining Sylvia had given him weeks before the snow set in.

The last argument Sylvia and Aunt Luella had took place on the front porch. It was the last time he saw his mother alive. Aunt Luella pointed her yellow finger in Sylvia's face, almost burning her with a cigarette. "You ain't shit. And you ain't never gon' be shit! Them streets done ate you up. Don't you care 'bout nothing no more?" Luella pulled her sweater up over her neck to fend off the wind. She turned her back to Sylvia.

Sylvia swayed from side to side to side. She tried to steady herself, but the cold air made her shiver. She wiped her nose. "I be trying. You know I be trying! I got my name on the list at Bethel. But, it's a two week wait. You know that."

"That boy eating up a lot of food, y'know? As long as that SSI keeps coming, he can stay. If it stops...you know I'm gon' have to give him back." She spoke to a frosted first floor window. Luella turned to face Sylvia. She was already half way down the stairs. She reached the bottom and slid her thin frame through the wrought iron gate. Peeking out of the second floor window, Jeremy saw her zigzag her way down Cicero, heading to the Marquis Room.

Homeboy

Roy, Eileen and Gladys had been in the psych ward all day it seemed. They watched Luther with anticipation and worry through the wall-sized glass window while he sat, staring at nothing. Then, he would get up every now and then to join the other patients, stumbling with baby steps like a two-year-old, afraid he would fall off the edge of the earth if he stepped too long. *At least he had on his own pants underneath his gown,* Eileen thought. He kept some dignity. The doctor and the therapist sat off to the side, leaning towards each other, whispering, pointing and writing notes.

"My fear, Mrs. Caldwell, is that the dementia might increase to a level that he could try to hurt himself. He keeps saying that he killed two people—problem is we don't really know if it's the dementia that's talking or just the meds." Dr. Omani rubbed his beard and squinted his eyes. He could have been speaking to both Eileen and Gladys.

The therapist spoke too. "He keeps talking about somebody named Harlan. Any of you know anyone by that name? It might be helpful if you did." He motioned towards Luther's wife, Gladys. "Anyone in Boston, maybe?"

Gladys wriggled in her seat, pressing so hard her tail bone felt as if it were naked and scraped against the chair's surface.

"No—no one I remember from Boston. I can't remember him saying anything about anybody from Chicago by that name. You think he might be the root of all this?" She reached back into her purse searching for another Altoid, but she really wanted a cigarette.

* * *

Luther drove slowly, south on Hamlin Street. If he had been a tourist, he'd have taken pictures. He cautiously avoided the broken glass left over from a summer's night and other debris scattered about. To his left, he could see the backdrop of the orange sun ball hovering over the block where his parents lived. It was still early morning. Chicago's Westside was just waking up—at least for the people who didn't come out at night. A patrol car with CHICAGO'S FINEST plastered on the side rolled past him in the opposite direction.Two cops—one white, one Black—pretended to look straight ahead, while typing in his license plate number. He knew they were checking him out, but they kept on going. His nervousness cooled.

His mind's eye suddenly became aware of everything, a sixth sense anyone who had grown up here was blessed with and never lost. It had become a mixture of gentrification and eyesore poured out of the glass, spilling and engulfing its surface—or an exquisite, expensive dinner that sits too long, waiting for someone to pick over it. The glassless windows of the six-flats stared down on him with dead, hollow, sunken eyes. His inner ear could hear the old vacant buildings speaking to him: Remember when you were born? When you bathed yourself in the lives of the people here? How many lives had they lived? How many pains they would give?

In 1967, things were different in Chicago, even in the Lawndale community. Even though the whites had long fled to the suburbs in response to a migration of Blacks from the south, grass still grew where there were now vacant lots. Beautiful, reddish-brown brick stood unmarked by the blood of tomorrow's turf warriors. People still had pride, he thought. After he had become a doctor and started making decent money, his parents still refused his offers to move them out and into Oak Park. Luther had always dreamt of becoming a doctor. Eventually, he left Lawndale to pursue those dreams. But as he found out years later, not everyone he grew up with would realize theirs. But he realized his and no one could ever take that away from him.

When he was little, he and his father moved along these streets without fear. It seemed like everybody knew his father, Roy. He was a laborer, a construction worker and had done masonry work on many of the buildings in the area. The butcher shop owner always gave Luther candy when he stopped by the store with his father. The butcher would make sure his family would get what was left of the best cuts of meat when they shopped on Fridays to buy for the following week. When they walked along Roosevelt, 16th and Central Park streets, Luther's short legs would struggle to keep up with the long strides his father took; he never missed a beat or tripped over broken sidewalk.

Roy would always point out the Black-owned businesses and smile. "See that, boy? That's what James Brown's talking bout!"

James Brown was still a mystery to Luther. Even though he'd heard the songs on the radio, it meant nothing to him. His father also pointed out the businesses that were fronted by black workers for white owners, too.

Eileen, Luther's mother, would usually stay at home on those days. She would ready the dinner that they'd eat about six o'clock that evening. When they'd return with the bags of groceries and newly cut heads, the house would smell of chicken, rice, gravy and biscuits. They never had to tell Luther twice to wash his hands and get seated at the table.

In the living room, an image of a Black Jesus looking upward hovered above whoever sat on the sofa bed beneath it. His parents argued over that, but his father had won out, citing chapter and verse, describing coarse hair and bronze skin. This didn't, however, affect his father's church attendance. They made sure Luther sat right next to them in pew number four every week at Greater Progressive. The building, a former Jewish synagogue, sat and served prominently on 16th and Lawndale. It was where Luther gathered his foundations. It was where he learned how his faith would carry him along in this journey. Sunday school, afterschool Bible study on Tuesdays and Thursdays, the teachings had never left—not even when he was asked to memorize all the books of the New Testament. Everyone on the block seemed to be there whenever anyone was served the rights.

Luther's own immersion into the water had the intended lasting effect he'd find later on in life. It wasn't the river, but it was close enough. He had bugged and bothered his mother for weeks until she relented and called Reverend Lindy and made arrangements. Luther thought he would be the center of the show that afternoon. But when he came to the church that Sunday afternoon and saw several other boys and girls his age lined up, he became jealous and refused to go through with it. Roy got wind of his recalcitrant mood change and threatened to make him do a holy dance that wasn't inspired by God's hands at all. Luther chose not to be embarrassed and ashamed and lined up right behind his best friend from fourth grade, Harlan.

Harlan could hardly contain his laughter, knowing about the *tête-à-tête* Luther and Roy had just gone through.

* * *

Luther's mother finally spoke, letting out secrets that everyone needed to hear. "Did you say Harlan, doctor?"

"Yes, ma'am. You know of this man, Harlan?"

Eileen shuffled her feet and crossed her ankles. "I don't know for sure, but the only Harlan I know of is from a long time ago. *Long time ago!* You remember that boy Luther played sports with?" She nudged her husband.

"I remember him. But I don't ever remember him causing Luther no trouble. Besides, I don't believe that boy is still alive. Y'know, a lot of them boys didn't make it through like Luther."

* * *

Luther smiled and hit the brake just as the light changed on him while he travelled home down that mental road. As he neared the middle of the block on Central Park where his parents stayed, it was close to 6 a.m. They were expecting him at 7. He knew his mother would be up anticipating his return. His father would pretend to be asleep. The old man was never one to show much emotion like that, but Luther knew that he cared. Sometimes too much. The sun was completely up. Its light changed and brightened his mood. Luther continued down Central Park corridor. Some of the porches leaned slightly one way or the other. As a child, he always fascinated himself with the smooth ones. Even though Roy had always worked with concrete and stone, it now tickled Luther that he had never asked him how in the world he and the other men got that stone so smooth and inlaid with a sculpture's delicate hand. Luther wondered if his father would think he was silly if he asked him now. He drove another twenty feet or so, pulled over to the curve, lowered his window and shut down the engine. He decided to just sit for a while.

He leaned his head back on the rest and lit another cigarette. *God, it has been so long,* he thought. Luther felt uneasy with the thought that this visit was different from the previous ones. The longest he had ever stayed over the years before were weekends and he only came because his mother wanted to see the grandkids. But what about all the times Gladys and the kids had to come alone while he stayed, because he didn't want to lose the money to be made from his private practice? He always felt bad about it, but never let on.

His programmed response, before putting on an album and turning up the volume to tune out Gladys' accusatory fussing was that, "He was only trying to make ends meet for his family." The only person who didn't understand was Gladys. They both knew that they had been growing apart for the last several years. It wasn't his intention—it just happened. What hurt him the most was a conversation between . Whenever Gladys and the kids left, Luther would stand in the front window, peeking through the curtain and drinking shots of JB scotch and soda, recalling how close they had been in college. Back then, on that campus, they had been telepathic close. Thinking each other's thoughts. Finishing each other's sentences. And finally, in his small dorm room, they'd wind up interlocked, naked, in a sleepy, emotional heap of perfumed sheets on the floor the next morning. They had been careful to use protection and didn't want children until they got married. Everything went as planned and they stood together, hand-in-hand, at Progressive's altar, while Reverend Lindy gave his blessings.

Gladys had been good for him. She had a sense of life, in the same way that his mother did. Her movements, speech and tastes were all her own, definite and graceful with a firm bottom that moved in rhythm from side-to-side underneath her skirt. Even after two kids, she still had it. A professional in her own right, she majored in business and was now a regional manager for a well-known retail clothing chain. Unlike Luther, Gladys had managed to keep her connection to the neighborhood in Boston where she had grown up. Three close friends from high school called her frequently and Luther found it hard to understand how that could be, considering their status and income. It was jealousy that fueled his questions, especially when the conversations went on for more than an hour at times. The small arguments then grew into big ones. Later, after they separated, alone with his thoughts and a drink, Luther admitted to himself that he was the one who usually started them.

This time, he wanted to stay awhile. Maybe go back up on 16th and Pulaski and see some of his high school buddies. Most he hadn't seen since the middle '70's and here it was 1989. The curiosity was killing him. Would they still remember him? Would they want to see him at all? He thought about how he had left and the fact that he had developed a reputation for being a mamma's boy. And since he had been an only child, he always got the best of everything that his parents could afford. They made sure of that. Luther heard the familiar sound of a ball pounding on the concrete and saw two young boys heading in the direction of Douglas Park. One of the boys dribbled, swiped the ball from hand to hand, stutter stepped, pulled up shooting an imaginary jump shot. Luther smiled and snubbed out the cigarette. He wanted to get out of the car and follow them, and then thought better of that idea. *Hell, Harlan and me? We would've showed those young boys something back in the day,* he thought. Luther and Harlan had played on the same teams since 6th grade.

They starred as a guard tandem—one of the best in the city. The faded image of Harlan and Luther lining up on defense while the other team took the ball out of bounds lightened his heart. Luther and Harlan had a routine that would've put a stop to that right away. Everyone feared it. They'd let the opposing guard catch the ball, get comfortable enough to start his dribble, let him cross the half court line and then they would swoop down from both sides. Either he or Harlan would fake a steal or block the passing lane. Arms spread wide; they'd jump up and down, scream and holler. The guard would get shook up and fumble his moves. They'd rip him off clean and start back down the court, doing exotic dribbling and throwing unnecessary passes back and forth to each other—just to turn on the crowd. For Harlan, the game was the only thing that mattered. He was by far the better of the two. Luther was good, but his game had its shortcomings, mainly his concentration. Harlan always made sure Luther was ready to play, teasing him just enough to get him mad so he could take it out on the other team.

Harlan was mean and muscular. His killer instinct would scare the shit out of half the teams they played just by staring at them during warm-ups. He called it his Westside stare. The crowd never distracted him—in fact, it turned him on. At Farragut High, Harlan loved breaking hearts with last second jumpers, steals and foul shots. His big rusty forearms made him a man-child. He had an instinct for the game. Everything came easy and so practice was usually a bore, just something that the coach insisted he do. Luther and the rest of the team always sat in amazement in the locker room before some games and watched as Harlan inhaled a McDonald's meal and not even flinch. He had an appetite like a monster. Many Friday evenings spent at Luther's house showed that Harlan wasn't ashamed when the team killed the table of pizza and chicken set out for them after a win. When they became seniors, several Big Ten colleges were hot on Harlan's trail, sending him letters and calling his house. Harlan's father didn't understand. He'd become enraged if the phone rang in the middle of his evening's rest. He'd answer and curse out the caller, then hang up. Harlan hated him for it. After graduation, he went on to Iowa State, but things just didn't work out. Harlan didn't want to develop his game. The coach told him he was spoiled, lazy and arrogant. After three semesters, he returned to Lawndale, broken, beaten and burned. Luther was long gone to Boston College. For Luther, basketball had become a pastime.

* * *

"If Harlan is still around, you think he talked to Luther?" Gladys chimed in hopefully.

"I doubt it," his father deadpanned. Even if we found him, ain't no way in the world Harlan would say anything that would get him in trouble."

"I would see him from time to time. Up at Walgreens. Hate to say but he'd be parked, selling stuff from his van. I mean, he'd speak. Never said or did anything wrong." Eileen insisted that Harlan was always respectful.

* * *

Through the windshield, Luther could see the yellowish light illuminate the curtain in the second floor bedroom window. He finally decided to get out of the car. He entered the gate and started up the front steps, before changing his mind and going around to the back porch. He stepped up quietly and slowly turned the key in the lock and entered. His mother had been watching him all the time in the front room window while he sat in his car. She continued to stand with her back to the door. Suddenly she turned around. "Luther Caldwell, don't you think you ought to speak when you enter a room?!"

Then, he hugged her, spinning her around the room with a laugh. "Well, I just thought I'd surprise you Mama, 'cause I know how you were always a stickler for time and being prompt."

"Well, let me look at you. You been eatin' right? Y'know if you went by Gladys' every..."

Luther cut her off. "Don't start on me, okay Mama? Anyway, where's the old man? It's almost 7:30. He should be up and around. He's been feeling okay, hasn't he?"

"Nothing wrong with me that a shot of Old Grand Dad couldn't cure. How's my boy? Life treating you right—still making that big doctor money?"

"I'm okay. You're looking good. Don't worry about the money. You and Mama spend enough of it."

Luther and his father laughed as they hugged each other. They both headed out the door to gather his bags from the car.

Luther waited until they were out of earshot of his mother. "So how's Mama? Is she still following her doctor's orders? You know I worry a lot about her?"

His father looked worried but tried to sound reassuring. "I don't know. She says she feels alright, but sometimes she looks

72

a little weak to me. I think that when you and Gladys called it quits that shook her up real bad. They talk on the phone all the time, y'know? Probably the best thing that could happen right now is if y'all tried it again."

"Look, I tried. I really did. But it seemed like we just couldn't make it."

"Reason it away if you want to, but I think your work did you in. You might clear three hundred grand a year, but all those hours of work cost you your family."

"Leave it alone, Dad. Just leave it alone."

His father heeded the warning. *As long as he knows how much it's hurting his mother*, he thought to himself.

Breakfast brought on a better mood, but before long, Luther became restless and impatient with his mother prying into his private life since the separation from Gladys. Unbeknownst to them, Luther knew they had separated briefly before he was born. His thoughts took him far away from the breakfast table but only for the moment. *Some men never bothered to hold up their responsibilities once the relationship was over—at least I did that!* he thought to himself. Every once in a while, Gladys would attempt to make him feel guilty and use the kids as a bargaining tool.

His father playfully slammed his palm on the table, shaking the coffee maker. "What's the matter with you, boy? You can't talk to your own people no more?"

"Huh?" Luther asked, startled.

"You look like you've got something on your mind, Luther," his mother asked. "Or are you just tired?"

"I don't know. I'm sorry. Everything feels kind of funny coming back here and not having to run back to Boston."

His mother looked at him reassuringly. She got up and stood

behind him. She placed her hands on his shoulders and began rubbing them. He relaxed a bit and thought about how she used to do that for him as a teenager. She knew just where to apply pressure to alleviate the tension. Luther relaxed and let his mother's long, slim hands work their magic.

"It's just the long drive, isn't it, son? Com'on, talk to me like you used to when your problems started to weigh you down."

Luther suddenly felt sleepy and wanted to lie down and rest. "I think I'd better go unpack and get settled in, Mama."

"Alright... but if you need to talk, you know I'm always here."

Luther got up from the table and stretched. He picked up his suitcases and headed down the short hallway for the bedroom. Once inside, he looked around. The beige paint still washed the walls. His bed was in the center. His dresser was still to the left of the window. Even the old Sears stereo that he had bought with his own money from his first job was still there. He wondered if it still worked. He placed his suitcases on the bed and took out some shirts to put in the dresser drawer.

On the side of the dresser lay three old Motown albums. The memories flushed through his mind. *What's Going On* held special meaning. He thought about the Vietnam War and the fact that he had just missed being drafted because of his acceptance into medical school. He decided to put it on the turntable. He wiped some of the dust off the plastic cover, opened it up and turned it on. He set the needle delicately on the record and sat down on the side of the bed and lay back. The music filled his mind. The bongo drums, saxophones and voices of a party moved through the room. His feet kept time with the beat. He thought about 16th Street, Douglas Park, Farragut High and all the faces and places that had become ghosts of his past. The music lulled him and he fell into a dream.

In the dream, he was standing on a corner. The faces that passed by mocked him as if they knew something he had yet to find out. Something inevitable and unavoidable. He tried to reach out and get someone's attention, but was ignored. Finally, he felt himself being lifted into the air. He was flying. He flew down Roosevelt Road, where he saw his first riot taking place. He remembered how stupid he felt at age eleven when Harlan had to explain to him why people were breaking windows and running down the street with clothes in their arms. He could hear Sly screaming about a riot going on. And there was.

Suddenly he became afraid. He wanted to fly further to get away from the chaos. But he just hung in mid-air. He couldn't move. All he could do was cry out for his mother as if he were a child. *Cry like a baby. Cry like a baby. All he could do was cry like a baby...*

Luther woke up and realized that he had been dreaming and sweating. The stereo was silent. The room was silent. He slowly raised himself up and tried to regain some composure. He looked at the clock. It was 10:30. He decided to finish unpacking. Afterwards, he would take a drive.

Luther stepped casually into the kitchen. The sun streaks through the window played on the counter top. For a moment he was caught up in its beauty. He poured himself some coffee and sat down at the table with his father. "So, Dad, give me the real scoop. What's really been going on?"

His father looked him square in the eyes. "I don't know. I'm worried."

"Worried about what? You didn't give me the whole story on Mom, did you?"

"I'm not so much worried about her as I am about you."

"Me? Please!" Luther answered, waving his father off. "I'm

okay—fit as fiddle. I'm a doctor, y'know?"

"And that's all you are. There's more to life than making money and driving a BMW, son. Think about it. You haven't been here on a visit for years. You've lost contact with everything and everyone here." Luther looked offended. "Look, I'm not telling you how to live your life. And it's not that your mother and me don't appreciate everything you're doing for us, but it seems like you've gone and left your roots, boy!"

Luther was stunned. He didn't know his father felt like this. He had heard this song and dance before, but never from him. He always thought that they were proud of him and what he had accomplished. The term "upwardly mobile" made him feel sick now.

Suddenly Luther got up from the table and headed for the screen door. His father tried to follow but couldn't catch up with him. Finally, he gave up and stood and watched as Luther sped off in his car.

* * *

"Maybe I shouldn't have said those things to him like I did the other morning," his father confessed.

"What things?" Eileen gave him a stare that drilled holes.

Mr. Caldwell stood, hiked up his pants and paced in definite steps like he always did when he wanted to be clearly understood. "Well, some things that..."

"What things!" Mrs. Caldwell's voice got louder and angrier.

"He was sitting there talking. Talking like everything was okay, how he was glad to be back and how he wanted to see his old friends and this and that. I told him he was dreaming. That he hadn't been here since I don't know when. And that those people don't remember him, don't know him anymore. And he don't know them either. He ain't ever had time for them before, not since he moved, so why now? I guess that set him off. After that, he went running out the door."

"And when were you going to tell me all this?" Mrs. Caldwell looked away with a hurtful look on her face.

"Like I say, some things between father and son ain't got nothing to... I mean..."

"Nothing to do with me, right?" Mrs. Caldwell got up and stormed out of the room. Gladys followed suit, giving her former father-in-law a look that said *you done done it now.*

* * *

Luther drove aimlessly. He was speeding and didn't realize it until he ran a red light and almost caused an accident. Heading down Madison Street with his mind still reeling from the scene with his father, he realized the further he drove, the worse the scenery would get. He approached Madison and Pulaski. He looked around at the stores and the people out in front of them. A depressing atmosphere hung in the air that seemed to say "since you are who you are, we can't offer you any better than this."

Luther drove on. He turned onto Pulaski, looking closely at every face he could see hoping that he would recognize one of them. He was determined to prove his father wrong. Finally, one looked familiar. Excited, he quickly pulled over to the curb, turned off the car and bolted out the door. "Harlan?" Luther yelled. "Harlan!"

He looked shorter than Luther thought he would. Some muscle still remained. Harlan was one of those bodies born with definition. His hands dangled at his side and still looked the same. Never completely open, but never completely closed. He always had big hands. He was one of the first in their group to palm a basketball. No one else could do it until they turned seventeen, but Harlan accomplished it at thirteen. The brother turned and squinted his eyes. Luther quickened his steps. Harlan stepped towards him cautiously. Then, Luther was close enough for Harlan to recognize.

"Well I'll be dipped in..." Harlan started laughingly.

"It's me, man! Luther... Luther Caldwell."

They reached out towards each other, then stopped. Luther didn't exactly know whether to hug him, offer the brothers' handshake or a standard one. Finally, they both seemed to call a truce and just stood there looking at each other.

Harlan spoke first. "It's been a long time, man. What brings you back here among us poor folk?"

Luther didn't know if Harlan was being playful or serious. So he took his chances. "Man, don't say that. I'm just glad to see you. So what you been up to? I guess you're married with kids now, huh?"

"Yeah, man, I went through that trip but, uhhhh... that was a while ago, y'know?" Harlan said this while he slowly ran his index finger under his nose and began to look around impatiently. Luther sensed his impatience and became unsure as to where this conversation might lead. "So what you been up to? Ever finish medical school? I guess you did, seeing what's parked over there?"

"I have my own practice in Boston."

"Boston!" Harlan said with faked excitement. "Tell you what, man... I got a couple of hours to kill. If you game, let's go over 'cross the street to the Marquis Lounge and catch up on old times."

"Sounds good to me," Luther replied.

They both made their way across the street to the Marquis. They walked through the door and sat down. Luther looked around as he ordered a scotch and soda. He was only used to drinking light dinner wine at this time of the day, always saving scotch for the evening. But he wanted to show he could hang.

Time passed and they continued the small talk, never really saying anything worth thinking about. The music was so loud they could barely hear anyway. Luther started to feel uneasy, because he had not been in this kind of atmosphere in years—a jukebox with a funky down home sound filling the air. He wouldn't have known how to dance to it if he was asked, but he found himself tapping his feet to the groove. The alcohol was getting next to him. He felt lighter, relaxed. *This is exactly the thing I had been running from ever since I left Chicago,* he thought to himself. He didn't feel himself to be arrogant, because he didn't drink rum and coke over a plate full of barbecue or drove a BMW and didn't owe a car note that was more than his rent. *These niggers don't know what they're missing. My standards and values are different from theirs. If I can afford to send my children to the better schools, why shouldn't I? So what if my speech patterns aren't full of slang, it's because I wanted to find and keep a job. I don't have to live like this. And no one can make me.*

Luther's reverie was broken by Harlan's old-school drooling. "Oooohweee! Baby, baby, baby! Do fries go wid that shake?"

Luther turned and looked. "Harlan, why don't you treat the lady with some respect? You wouldn't want anybody talking like that to your own sister, would you?"

Harlan's frowned and curled his forehead. "Who died and made you God? That drink must've done more to yo' brain than

79

you planned on. You don't know me like that! Let me tell you something about sisters, in case you forgot... they like that shit, man. See, it ain't got nothing to do with no disrespect. She wouldn't be showing no leg like that if she didn't want to get hollered at. But you probably ain't had no pussy like that since high school. What's the matter? All those rich white bitches up in Boston got you working overtime, baby?"

Luther put his drink down. "Look man, I thought this was supposed to be a good time? I'm not down on your ethics—don't get down on mine. Besides, I don't see how you could stand to be in such a disgusting place like this. Half these niggers should be in school or at work somewhere. But they are here, because—like you—they chose to be here. Blame *that* on the white man!"

Harlan frowned. "Well, lookey here. We done gone and sold the farm. Y'know, I's sorry we don't meet yo' standards Hoss, but we's just been worrying our po' little heads off down here in the ghetto. Oh, I fo'gets. This is the URBANE AREA now!"

Luther was ready to tear Harlan's head off in defiance. He stormed out of the bar, but almost fell out from the high heat and humidity once outside. He stumbled across the street where he was parked, but was stopped dead in his tracks with disbelief. His car was gone. Luther panicked, spun around and ran back over to the bar to see if he could get Harlan's help.

He swung the doors open with full force, but there was no sign of Harlan. *That son of a bitch!* he thought.

The bartender looked at him suspiciously. "What's up, man. Can I help you with something?"

"You remember that guy I was sitting at the bar with?" Luther asked, out of breath. "You know where he went?"

"You mean Harlan? Man, he hit the back door soon as you hit

the front. I'll tell you what though it's pretty close to twelve. He's probably at his old lady's, getting his daily dose. Name's Irma. If you run, you might be able to catch him. Harlan don't stay in one place too long."

"Where can I find Irma? I need to know now, man!"

"She's about four blocks down on 13th Street. When you get to the forty hundred block, just ask anybody sitting out front. They'll show you. It's a two-flat."

"Thanks, man," Luther said, rushing out the door.

The summer heat beat down on him hard. He wished he was still at home in Boston, sitting in his apartment under the air conditioning, watching television. He wished he had never come back.

Not back to this, he thought. *These thieving ass niggers don't deserve nothing. They always want to take something from someone else. The man who used to be my best friend stole from me.*

He turned the corner at 13th and slowed his walk, so he could see the addresses better. "Thirty-nine, forty," Luther counted under his breath. He saw a man sitting on a porch. He was an older man who looked much like his own father—retired and waiting out the days.

"Excuse me, sir. Could you tell me where a woman by the name of Irma lives?"

The old man glanced at Luther and adjusted his glasses. "Depends on who's looking for her. You don't look like you're from around here."

"I don't mean her any harm, sir. I'm just trying to locate another friend of mine. And they said he might be with her."

The old man looked again. "That face of yours looks familiar, but I can't seem to place it off hand."

"Name's Luther, Luther Caldwell. I used to live around here

81

as a young boy. My parents are Eileen and Roy."

The old man's eyes lit up. "Eileen and Roy! Douglas and Central Park, right? Me and your father used to work together, doing masonry and such. Is he still alive? How's he doing these days..."

Luther didn't want to seem rude but he had had enough of this cat and mouse game and cut him off. "I really need to know that house, sir... if you could help me."

"Oh sure, she lives right 'cross the street there. See the house with the blue shades?"

Before he could finish, Luther was in the middle of the street heading towards the steps. Luther watched the shades to see if they moved. If they did, he figured Harlan might be looking out for him. He walked briskly up the stairs and rang the doorbell. Luther stood and glared impatiently. He began to think about his childhood. He looked behind him and realized that the vacant lot where he and Harlan built their first sandcastles was now used for parking. He saw himself and others playing on the swings in the summertime. At the other end of the lot, the older boys were cursing and laughing while shooting dice. The older boys were always getting into something. He thought about the time he and Harlan were scared shitless one hot summer night. They were running through the alley playing hide and seek and were suddenly confronted by a man who lived next door in an apartment building. He was drunk and holding a gun, leaning from side to side. He seemed like a giant to them at the time. His processed hair was slicked back like a wet mop. They had seen him work on cars in the in the lot behind the building. Maybe that's why he "was looking for those niggers who were always messing around and stealing battries." Luther laughed to himself when he thought about how he had nightmares about the man flying into a rage, shooting him and Harlan, leaving them for dead in the alley. He thought about his own son and his first nightmares.

Finally someone peeked through the curtains on the doors. "Who is you?"

"Uh, my name is Luther Caldwell and I am looking for Irma. Is she in?"

"She lives on the second floor. You rang the wrong doorbell."

Luther started to thank her, but the curtain flew back into place before he could finish. Exasperated, he reached up and pressed the other doorbell. Time passed and then he heard footsteps. Through the curtain, he could barely make out a figure dressed in a nightgown. She peeked through the side of the curtained window and then opened wide enough to reveal only her face.

"Yeah, can I help you?" she asked, inhaling a cigarette.

"Hi, my name is Luther Caldwell. And I'm looking for a guy named Harlan. I was told he might be here."

"Listen, before you go tearing up my house, I ain't seen nor heard of that nigger. And if you see him, tell him I wants my money. What he done stole of yours? From the looks of you, it must be something expensive."

Expensive? Luther thought. *I sure don't see too many BMWs parked around here.* "No, you listen! I'm missing my car. I'm not for any more fun and games you niggers around here like to play. I think you know where he is and I want you to tell me—now!"

Without thinking, Luther pushed his way through the door and dragged her up the steps. She pleaded with him to let her go, but it did no good. He was in a rage. They reached the top of the staircase and entered the apartment together. Luther threw her against the wall and looked around. The place was almost empty. Alongside the couch sat a coffee table. In the middle of the table was a pipe and other paraphernalia.

"Look, you crackhead bitch... tell me where he is or I'll break your neck!"

"I'm telling you. I don't know. I haven't seen him in the last two months. Sometimes he'll hang out with them boys down the street in the gallery. He used to come by here every once in a while to mess around. But I don't smoke no more, so he don't have the time, y'know?"

"You're lying! I know what that stuff is on the table over there. This ain't no B movie."

Before Luther could continue, Harlan appeared from the back bedroom with a gun in his hand. They stood and glared at each other. Luther saw the gun but didn't care. Here he was, a fifty-year-old Black professional who had spent years trying to move on up, suddenly caught up in the middle of a ghetto cliché. A black professional, who ate at the best restaurants, bought the best clothes, drove the best cars and rubbed shoulders with college professors now in a crossfire with the very people he thought he was too good to be around.

Luther moved first, edging slowly towards Harlan.

"Look man, all I want is my car. You can have your life. I'm sorry I intruded. All I want is what's mine."

"What's yours? Man, you don't own nothing! You don't own nothing in this world! What good is all that status gonna do you when death comes knocking on your door? You know what the old folks say: come here with nothing, leave here with nothing. You think you too good to be around us? Let's see if you too good to die around us too."

Harlan raised the gun and took aim. Luther knew he had to move fast. He grabbed the door which was still ajar and swung it completely open. Surprised, Harlan only got off one round. But before he knew it, Luther had landed a solid right to his jaw. Harlan dropped the pistol and went down to one knee. Luther grabbed for the gun. He had it in his grasp and hit Harlan flush on the side of his face with it. Harlan went down hard on the floor. Luther bent over him breathing hard. Blood trickled down Harlan's face. Luther looked at the gun. Then he looked at Harlan. Luther's fingers trembled as he tried to act as if he knew how to handle a gun.

Rage and violence swelled up in him. Luther used to wonder if put in the position to kill someone, would he? He never planned on having to make a decision like this. He never planned on having control over life and death—someone else's life, someone else's death! He began to understand that he, Harlan and all the blacks in this world still stood on common ground. If pushed to the limit, even he could revert to the survival level he had strived so hard to leave. If he pulled the trigger, he could spend the rest of life in jail. If he didn't pull the trigger, would the things Harlan spoke of turn out to be true? All his adult life, he had chased the dream. All of his adult life, he had asked for nothing more than to not be categorized as a typical nigger.

Luther began to squeeze the trigger. The sweat on his hand made it slippery. The sweat on his face ran down like a waterfall. His eyes burned furious holes into Harlan's who returned his own incensed gaze.

"Kill me!" Harlan spat out. "Are you man enough? I'm nothing but a dumbass nigger, smoking dreams—the disaster you run from. Nothing but one of those sad characters created by the media."

Suddenly, Luther dropped the gun and relief appeared on Harlan's face. He was bluffing after all. Harlan was glad but confused. Luther began to laugh. A laugh of irony and relief. "My father was wrong. I don't have to prove a damn thing to you or any of these other niggers." Luther rose from the floor. Like the Phoenix rising from the ashes. Like a child taking his first steps. Everything anew. Luther gave the gun to Harlan and started to turn away.

Harlan looked at Irma and smiled. "This man done lost his mind."

Luther turned again with his voice cracking. "It's okay, man. It's okay." Harlan stood there with a look of amazement on his face, but somehow felt he understood. He and Irma watched Luther as he walked slowly down the steps mumbling to himself—something about still being a homeboy.

* * *

"I guess he's lost his mind." Mr. Caldwell shook his head from side and stamped his foot on the floor, dabbing his eyes with his handkerchief.

"He must have made all of this up. Sometimes people do that y'know, especially when they try to create a reality that's really not there." Dr. Omani tried to be consoling. "From what his wife says, he's been working a 70-hour work week for years. That's too much, even for a doctor. I have a few friends in Boston. They work at the hospital. They will keep it under wraps, okay? Six months of therapy will do the trick. He will be back in no time."

Bluesman

U ncle John was a soul man. As long as I could remember, he played the blues. His long, spidery, calloused brown fingers sliding up and down the frets walked a familiar road, a road laid years ago. We would sit on the old beat up sofa in the front room and he'd begin to play and sing.

Mama Sayra would always holler from the kitchen. "Johnny, quit fillin' that boy's head with all that country stuff! This is the city!"

Uncle John would snort, knowing she didn't mean no harm and holler right back. "Boy's got to learn his roots, Sayra!" Then, Uncle John would begin to wail softly on his twelve string.

I was raised on Maxwell Street, a place sometimes called Jew Town in Chicago. The people there sang its immigrant song. Ever since Uncle John and Mama Sayra had come from Mississippi, he had been singing the blues. He tried to explain every song he sang to me. To hear Mama Sayra tell it, Uncle John stood over my crib when I was a newborn and sang a soft blues to bless me and lullaby me to sleep. Mama Sayra would get wind of what he was doing and come to run him out of the room. Uncle John had built quite a reputation as a bluesman around Chicago from the late forties to the late sixties.

"Son, the blues is yo' legacy," he would always say when I got older. "Don't neva let it go. It's yo' roots, the river that flows in yo' bloodline from here to Mississippi!" Then he'd dip his snuff and spit into the Crisco can he kept by the side of his easy chair.

Sometimes, he would walk me home from school. We would always stop by Mr. Gibbons' store to buy me candy and make me swear not to tell Mama Sayra. No matter how many times we would walk down the same block, past the same buildings, people, trees, businesses and lots, Uncle John would find something interesting that I hadn't noticed the day before. He walked with a staggered stroll, trying not to step on a line. He said it would be bad luck if he did. Even though this was the city, he'd point out something about the way the sun shone that day or the way the weeds and grass grew. And we'd always hear the soft and heavy blues sounds sifting out through someone's window. Or maybe another blues man would be sitting on the street corner, strumming away. If he were, his guitar case would be open. Pennies, nickels, dimes and quarters lay silently sprinkled on the inside felt covering. No matter what, the bluesman would tip his hat towards me and Uncle John with reverence, paying tribute.

Uncle John had a sixth sense that was unmatched. He could tell so many things about people just by looking at them. It was as if he could read your mind. "The peoples is the stories of my songs. I can tell the troubling or the happy times in a man's mind just by looking in his eyes."

One day, he could sense that something was troubling me. "Nothing!" I replied and kicked a flattened Budweiser can into the street. Uncle John placed his long thin hands on my shoulder and gripped it hard. He'd always nudge and dig the truth out of me until I finally gave in. "Well, Tommy... Tommy said that you never played the blues or traveled with Muddy Waters and John

Lee Hooker. He said his daddy said so."

Uncle Johnny smiled and released his grip. "And what'd you say, Michael?"

I frowned and clenched my fist. "I told him his daddy didn't know nothing and if he kept on talking..."

Uncle John interrupted. "Then Miss Lane got in between the both of you, huh?" He took a deep sighing breath, got that far away look like he had when he was down sick and Mama Sayra was taking care of him. We stopped and waited for the red light to change. "Listen, Michael, that's not the way to handle conflic'. You hear what I'ma saying? You cain't make nobody b'lieve anything if they don't wants to!" He began to chew on his cigar in his usual deliberate way. "I 'member one time, way back 'fore you was born. Me and yo' Mama Sayra had a conflic'. A conflic' 'bout that very thing, 'blieving what peoples say is true. I couldn't been no more than nineteen. She was round twenty-five. I come running in the house one evening. High strung as a young colt. See, I'd met up this young white fella. He call hisself a record man and say he like the way I sings and wanted me to make one of them plastic records."

"But why wouldn't Mama Sayra like that?" I asked.

"See, yo' Mama Sayra raise' me after Big Mamma passed on—that's yo' great grandma. Yo' mamma was always looking out for my well-being. She promised Big Mamma, when she was on her death bed that she'd look after me—keep me outta trouble and such. But she knowed how much I liked playing the blues. I b'lieve she wanted me to do good, but she didn't want me to go down that crossroads and get hurt."

"The crossroads? What's that?"

Uncle John smiled to himself, chewed his cigar and rolled it from side to side. "That's 'nother story. See, she didn't b'lieve me when I tole her that man wanted me to sign that paper I held so tight in my hands."

"What happened? Did Mama Sayra believe you when you showed her the paper?"

Uncle John laughed and shuffled his feet. "Naw, she didn't b'lieve me! But she come around 'bout six months later when I came home off the road and showed her my record. Big as day, a picture of me an' my guitar! Lawd, her mouf just dropped to the floor!"

My mood brightened. "Did she believe you then?"

Uncle John skipped, stepped and clapped his hands. "Sho' she b'lieve me! See what I'ma trying to tell you is that sometimes you just have to make yo' say, put it in yo' own heart, know that it's true and gone on an' prove it to peoples. You gone on back in the morn' and don't pay no mind to what that boy say 'bout me. Long as *you* know what's the truth."

Later on that evening, I lay in my bed while the cool spring air swirled in from my window. I could hear Uncle John's soft, moaning blues stream in from the kitchen. Like always, I knew he'd have a pot of coffee simmering on the stove, his pipe and tobacco lying on the table, the lamp light dimmed to his satisfaction and a blues prayer in his heart.

Years later, I'd replay that walk home from school with him over and over in my mind. It was that piece of my roots that Uncle John told me to keep. I have kept it and never let it go. The blues is magic and Uncle John walked in its golden light. He impressed upon me that my legacy is important and I couldn't afford to let it die.

As I stood over his coffin and looked at his remains, other thoughts of Uncle John filled my soul. Mama Sayra sat on the pew, wiping her eyes every now and then. But I know that there was joy inside her tears. "Uncle Johnny served his time and gone on home," she said solemnly.

I tried not to cry, but couldn't help it. I felt better after I let some tears flow. There was no sadness in my heart. I thought of Uncle Johnny as I always did: like a guardian angel. He'd never leave my spirit because he had left a part of his. Uncle Johnny's memory was like the unchanging portrait that hung on the wall at home. And I know that he would be proud of me and Johnny Jr.

Spirit

The carriage wheels shook, leaning from side to side between the maples leafs. Rufus rode the horses as hard as he could. He sweated through his clothing and felt bad for lashing the horses so violently. Out the corner of his eye, he spied Dr. Johnson's worried, nervous looks and knew what he was thinking. The adventure had started so suddenly, their dalliances—his lusting, his fantasizing, and ultimately his tasting of her exotic, dark skin. She had come on the ship with all the others. She stood there, shining and naked, in an unholy lineup, waiting to be taken by the highest bidder. He was only looking to replace stock that had grown older. The first temptations were subtle and Johnson tried to shrug them off as natural and physical. He hadn't planned on sampling the forbidden nectar of color, forsaking his wife and family and drowning himself in it.

The doors of the mansion groaned and leaned inward in a bursting motion with each pound by the men on the other side. On the side of the mansion, the slaves nervously looked on and whispered among themselves. "She gone do it! Lawd! Hep us an' dat po'gal in dere. We prayin', Lawd! We prayin'."

Dr. Johnson and the town's other white men grunted with every thrust and cursed each time their log hit the barred oak doors. Dr. Johnson's wife stood to the side, wailing through her tears as the other white women tried to comfort and console her.

Inside the mansion, upstairs in the bedroom, Mary held her baby boy in cupped hands. She prayed and spoke in tongues as her hands lowered slowly into the tub of water. The child's arms splashed in the water and reached upwards as it filled his mouth, nose, lungs, ears and eyes. His angelic, tan-brown face distorted as the water covered him like dirt on a grave. Finally, after the boy's face had turned blue, the deed was done.

"Ho Gloray!" Mary screamed, before letting loose her tears, knowing that his life had gone. She turned and slumped onto the floor just as Dr. Johnson and the other men burst in through the door. Mary moved into a trance, crying incoherently. "Ain't gon' make my baby no slave!"

Dr. Johnson struck her repeatedly with a large stick. "You nigger wench! Your black ass gon' hang for this! That's my blood you killed!" Three of the other men finally restrained him long enough to take the stick away from him.

Night fell like a blanket of snow. It was heavy, laden and silent. The only sound heard came from the north pasture where the slave women moaned a soft spiritual and prayed for the souls of Mary and her child.

Mary's body twisted and twitched in the blowing wind—her brown-black nakedness shadowed by the red-orange ball of sun. Dr. Johnson told the slave preacher that Mary could not be taken down for three days. He proudly announced on slave row that Mary should serve as a reminder to all nigger wenches on the plantation: breed and live, defy and die.

* * *

"Y'all know, John, dis heah land used to be where dat plantation stand?"

John shot a killing look at Henry. "Look, don't go startin' that ghost stuff. I got a wife an' kids heah, y'know?"

Henry eyed the ground and shuffled his feet. "I don't mean no harm. I'ma just sayin'..."

John held up an open hand. "Just don't say nuttin', ya heah?"

"Brotha John ain't nobody startin' nuttin'," Henry argued further. "You knows the histry! For the last hunnerd years, dat baby's an' his mama's spirits been floatin' 'round sumpin' fierce. Heah tell, if'n you lissen real close at night, you can heah 'em both cryin' up a storm. Cain't no spirit find no rest lef' like they was lest they finally make co'nection wid a livin' human. Powerful, powerful spirits! You just gots to be careful. Folks say the Johnson family ain't been right since dat day back in 1832. What dat Granddaddy done to dat woman cursed the whole family fo' years—mebbe to this very day. Now, I sees his grandson spending' all his time givin' his family's money to us colored, openin' up schools an' ever'thin'."

John had heard just about enough. "Look, all we done was buy some lan', built up a home an' I ain't gon' let you or no spirits scare me!"

Henry continued to press the issue. "Still an' all, betta let Rev Sizemore say a blessin' fo' the month is out to be on the safe side."

Later that evening, John moved nervously throughout the house. His wife Mae noticed and called to him from the front porch. "John, is you okay?"

"Yeah, just checking on the chil'ren," John answered quickly.

Mae didn't believe him. "You checked a half an' hour ago. You is 'sposed to be sittin' out heah wid me!"

John stepped heavily, pushing the screen door outward, walking over to the railing and propping a foot up on it. "Mae?"

"Wha's on yo' min', John?"

"You reckon we oughta call ole Rev up?"

"Call the Rev. fo' what? You ain't sick, is you?"

"Naw, I ain't sick!"

Mae grew impatient. "What then?"

"I don't know. It's just dat Henry."

Mae let out an exasperated sigh when she heard Henry' name. Even though he was her brother-in-law, Mae had never liked him. He talked too much about things he knew nothing about. Whenever Henry and his family would come over, Mae would always stay within earshot of him and the kids, so she could interrupt anytime he'd start to scare them half to death with some story or legend he'd heard. When Henry would start in, Mae would offer up some homemade ice cream and the kids would gravitate towards her like bees to honey.

She arose from her seat and patted and smoothed her flowered dress. "John, what dat Henry done gone and filled yo' head up wid now?" John turned and slowly walked to the side of the porch. "I knows what it is. It was dat story 'bout dem spirits, ain't it? Henry wouldn't know the sun was shinin' if'n nobody tole him."

The last remark angered John. "Mae, ain't no call to go an' talk lak dat 'bout my brotha. He might be a little on the slow side, but he still my brotha, y'know."

Mae softened her words. "I doan mean no harm. I knows Henry wouldn't hurt a fly, John. But let me tell you sumpin' 'bout those spirits, sumpin' my granny tole me when I was yea high."

"Wha's dat?" John asked with a worried look.

"When I was little, my mamma say she an' the family was alway worryin' an' watchin' on me. 'Specially at night, when the spirit come. But my granny knowed wasn't nothin' wrong. She tole me dat the spirit always choose a little chile to reveal themself to. Dey doan mess wid adults 'cause adults is too 'fraid of dem. Only chilren unnerstand dem. Mamma used to have a fit when Granny got to preachin'. Mamma say *'ain't no need in gettin' dat chile rile up o' no spirits!'* But Granny wouldn't quit. I guess she knowed what she was talkin' 'bout."

John still disagreed. "Ain't nobody got no business messin' wid no chile o'mines!"

Mae smiled knowingly. "John ain't nothin' none of us can do 'bout it. De spirit come when dey come."

John gave up. He looked at Mae and shook his head in disbelief. But in the weeks to come, John would keep a keen eye on Lilly, their youngest daughter who was almost four. One night, John was restless and couldn't sleep. So he decided to make a check on the family late one night. While walking through the hall towards the children's bedroom, he heard a strange noise coming from the attic up above. The sound of little feet moving excitedly about. John didn't waste any time deciding to see who or what was up there. He tiptoed softly up the several steps leading to the darkened room. The door was ajar. Quietly, he peered through and around the door's opening. What he saw almost gave him a heart attack. There was Lilly seated at a small, round table. On the table was the tea set given to her last Christmas. The cups and saucers were strategically placed as though there were at least two other people sitting on the other side, but John saw only Lilly. She spoke so softly that John could not make out her words. She made motions with the teapot as if she were serving her invisible visitors. John wanted to say something, but the words would not come. He could not speak. Finally, he turned around quietly and made his way back down the steps without disturbing the floor boards. He walked to the end of the hallway, stopped and peered out of the window and into the star-filled, deep blue night sky.

Calm and quietness filled his heart. He began to breathe easier, no longer nervous or scared. "Lord's will be done," he said to himself softly before turning to go back to his bedroom.

Tang

Tang's funeral was a quiet hoot, as far as I was concerned. It was at John Nash's place on Stony Island in the morning.

The preacher sat looking down on the audience and obligatory congregation members, ushers and a nurse. They were ready at the pastor's nod to rush up to the front with Kleenex and a small throw if needed. The pastor knew from experience at least one of the family would start to feel guilty, feign grief and fall out. Tang's family was one of those, the pastor thought. Everybody thought Tang was no good. But, it wasn't his fault. He didn't have a Daddy and hardly had a Mama. Grandma had always cried over him.

The mortician was nice, but I didn't trust him. Grandma was tired and saying yes to everything he suggested. When I would ask him how much, he would let out a sigh and go into a long lecture about how he always took care of the families around here, but I kept pressing the issue. Finally, he gave two prices. I nudged Grandma when he said the lower one. It was settled. We'd let Uncle Sam do whatever he needed and give Tang all the rights and privileges coming to him. Uncle Sam was footing the bill anyway.

Grandma cried over Tang when he first left for Vietnam at

18. Tang smiled at the door with his bag in his hand heading for Quantico, Virginia. The first letter Grandma got from him was full of tears. Then, Grandma went to church and made sure she gave Tang's name to the secretary to pass on to Reverend Harris so he could pray a special prayer for Tang. It must have worked because three years later, Tang came back home. He wasn't completely whole though. His right hand hung loosely from his wrist. Later, when Grandma took him to the doctor, she found out that Tang had tried to throw a hand grenade back where it came from and had his hand blown off.

Not knowing what else to do, Tang looked around for it and found it laying on the ground, jumping around like a frog. He picked it up and held on to it until the medics came. The nurse was horrified when he pulled it out of his pocket and showed it to her. The nurse doubled the morphine and Tang blacked out. When he woke up in the makeshift infirmary, he looked down and saw that the doctors had sewn his hand back onto his wrist. Later that day, Tang's sergeant told him he was going back to the world, so he'd better get ready. I imagine Tang was still in a drug-induced world trying to make out the sergeant's words. One thing for certain, Tang would have to teach his left hand to do what his right had been doing for years.

* * *

Grandma always says "Oh, Jesus!" She prays for everybody, at least everybody in the building. She's lived in this court way building for going on forty years. It's the only place I ever remember living. Since then, there'd been two major renovations, one in 1985 and the other in 2000. Grandma always goes to church and she says that that the renovations is proof that Jesus heard her prayers.

Where's Jesus when you need him? But Grandma says He's always around even when you don't see Him. He sees all and knows all. And if that isn't enough, He might come back like a thief in the middle of the night and grab the whole world and shake it up.

In the first row, I overhear my aunties whispering about the insurance money Grandma is going to get in a few weeks and how they better start going over there, helping her out. But I know Grandma won't be fooled. She'll sit there in the living room, rocking back and forth, looking away every once in a while like she's really listening. My aunties will just keep on talking nervous like, hoping Grandma won't drop the hot question: where was y'all when Tang needed somebody?

Tang's favorite color was sky blue. I always liked that and that's why I dragged Grandma up to Madison and Pulaski to shop for a sky blue suit to bury Tang in. Grandma said she didn't know that was his favorite color. Grandma said he never told her that, but if that's what Tang said it was, then that's what it was. She was always matter of fact like that. It was just like the cheap costume jewelry necklace Tang bought her for her birthday when he was fourteen and got his first job. Tang told her it was the only one in the world like it. Grandma still has it and takes it out of her dresser drawer every now and then.

By now, the Reverend had started his ritual. He deadpanned the family every few minutes or so and looked at his watch. I wonder if the reverend even knew anything about Tang. How Grandma and me found that letter from the marines stuffed in the back of his dresser. Wrapped up in the letter was a medal of honor from the marines. The letter said it was to show appreciation for his bravery, protecting his platoon from that grenade explosion. We never knew he had it. What we did know was how Tang would disappear for days sometimes. Then come back home disheveled and hungry. Grandma always had a plate of something ready for him. Sometimes Grandma would send me and my best friend Julia downtown to look for him. We always knew where to go—underneath the El at State and Van Buren, a stop across the street from the library.

When Grandma went to the hospital to get his belongings, the doctors told her how Tang kept mumbling something about the gargoyles on the corner of the roof of the library were swooping down to get him. It really shook me up when Grandma said that. Among his other belongings were the jeans he always wore, a blue sweat shirt, the brown-grayish jogging shoes we got him for his last birthday, and a black skull cap he loved dearly. The back pack was another issue. Tang carried his whole life in that back pack and rolling suitcase, big enough to strap on a folding lawn chair, his guitar and a portable chalk board that I could never figure out where he got that from. Tang couldn't play the guitar. He'd just strum it. He had it since high school and Grandma kept it for him when he went off to war.

Now it seems like Tang had a whole 'nother life. Time can make you wise or it can make you a fool. The honey can be sweet or it can be bitter. It all depends on how you drink it in. I don't think Tang ever really felt comfortable in his suit. Confused, mad, paralyzed, shocked, depressed? Tang was all of those things and then some. The reverend never really said whether they had prayed or what he and Tang had talked about when he went to see him at Grandma's insistence. But Reverend Harris said Tang was alright now—and that was enough for me.

Evil In The World

Lucien bounded down the stairs and slammed the heavy wooden door behind him. He had to be careful when he got to the bottom of the first flight of stairs, because there was a steep flight of sixteen outside that led directly down to the sidewalk. To him, the outside staircase was special. It was where part of his early education took place. Evening after evening, night after night in the summertime, he and his older brother and several of their friends would play a game called School. This usually entailed answering a question—usually by making a guess—and choosing which hand held a rock that would allow him move up one step. If he guessed the answer to a question correctly, he could move up an extra step. Sometimes, because he was so young, his brother would let him slide and pass. The others understood and approved without letting on that they knew what was going on. He always had fun. The only thing that bothered Lucien was that his questions would never be as sophisticated or complicated as his brother's. Someone would answer his question right away and move up. Still, most of the time, his age did not allow his brother to have mercy on him. He would chide Lucien, just to let him know that "knowing" was better than "not knowing." It didn't pay to be stupid—not on this earth.

"How many pounds make up a ton?" his brother commanded with a sarcastic smirk, knowing Lucien could not answer.

Lucien looked away. "I don't exactly know."

"Stupido!" his brother would snap back, imitating the foreign soldiers that they had seen on film at the movies. "Two thousand! Go down one step." Years later, Lucien would realize it was his way of preparing for the harsh realities of life. The relationship Lucien had with his brother was one of nurturing and closeness. He never let Lucien out of his sight when they were outside. Lucien watched and learned.

Whenever the signifying would start amongst their friends, nobody wanted to go up against Markus. It was his vocabulary that everyone feared. Most of it, Markus had garnered from comic books and other literature that he constantly read. "Never without a book" was his motto, and very seldom did they see him without one. He had a knack for remembering and using big words to insult his peers, without their realizing it. God help them if they made the mistake of signifying back at him. He'd light into them with a barrage of words like a machine gun gone out of control. Then, they'd stand there bewildered, seething and burning up inside as they watched him grin that ghoulish, toothy grin and show his white teeth. Afterwards, tall, dark and slender Markus would stand straight and stare with his hands in his pockets, daring someone else to say something in rebuttal.

Lucien bopped and stepped briskly down the stairs. Every now and then, he'd pat his right pocket, checking to see if his nickel was still there. Couldn't lose that nickel, especially since it took him all of an hour, sitting at his mother's knee begging for it. He knew she would eventually give in. She spoiled him because he was still the baby of the family. She taught him lessons too—that one couldn't get everything, all the time, right away.

His mother's tall body was encased in caramel skin and she had long legs that were strong. Protruding from her hands were long fingers, the same ones that kneaded his favorite biscuits at the kitchen table. Once, when at his usual spot on floor leaning his head against her knee, he noticed that there were three brown spots on her leg that went upward from her ankle to her calf.

Always inquisitive, he asked, "Mama, what's that?"

She smiled. There was a far off look in the eyes. "When I was a little girl still down home, me and my sisters were running back home, trying to get in before a storm."

Lucien was enraptured. "And then what happened?"

"Well, I could see it coming through the trees. The lightning had been raging for a while. And all of a sudden it hit."

"Hit you?"

"Hit a tree branch first. Then, it snaked its way down to me. When I woke up, I was at home. Everybody was standing over me, praying. Every since the doctor took the bandage off, the spots been there. They healed up and that was it."

"Did it hurt?"

"Don't remember."

Lucien sighed and squinted his eyes and kept on watching the TV screen.

Sensing a letdown, Mama patted the top of his head and rubbed his hair. "You'll learn as you get older."

At the bottom of the stairs, Lucien made a right turn and headed in the direction of the corner store. Usually, one of his family members would be with him. Every once in a while, when his sister would get desperate for some hosiery and couldn't find anyone else willing to go, she'd break her mother's rule and send him down to Mr. Joe's Store with the money wrapped up in a hand-scribbled note.

The owners were white. He and his wife were Jewish hangers-on from the Westside neighborhood that had gradually turned Negro in the early 1950's after the war. There was a billboard down the street that stood watch from on high with a likeness of Willie Mays hawking brand-name syrup. Lucien just assumed that Joe and his wife had been and would always be a part of the scenery. Usually he, his brother and his friends would all gather together after school on Fridays and run over to the store to buy as much penny candy as they could. Joe would stand behind the counter, following the finger-pointing ritual that Lucien and the others would go through. Joe pretty much remained cordial and silent, except when his wife would shuffle out from the back of the store and speak to him in a low voice. He would nod intensely, and motion towards the curtained doorway that led to the back. Without a sound, she would turn and leave. Sometimes she would look at the kids and smile and Joe would continue his task of serving the kids. Trying not to be noticed, Lucien would stare at the strange etchings on a plaque on the wall, the same Hebrew language he'd seen on the cornerstone of the church he and his family attended every week. Once, Lucien got up enough nerve to ask one of the deacons what it was and what it meant. Even though he so young, he could sense how flustered and embarrassed the man looked, attempting to cover up with a story and that he didn't really know or couldn't explain it fully.

Everyone looked tall to Lucien and Joe was no different. He was in his late sixties pale-skinned and slender with thin, grayish black hair. He never smiled, yet was always polite. The only time he would see Joe in a bad mood was when the older teenagers came in to shop. He didn't trust them and they knew it.

One day, Lucien was sitting on the bottom step of the porch by himself, scraping a broken tree limb across the concrete and chasing the brown ants that scrambled around. Suddenly, he looked up and saw several of the older boys from the block, tearing ass down the street, carrying bread, milk and other items under their arms. Although he was a little afraid, Lucien looked down the street towards the store. He saw Joe leaning outside of the doorway of his store, flailing his arms and screaming obscenities in a language that he did not understand. When Lucien told Markus what happened, he explained that they did a bad thing, and to never do that to Joe, because he and his wife were good people and had been through a lot, long before he was born. Lucien tried to quiz him further, but Markus wouldn't give in. He simply said that some of the things he was talking about, they had seen at the movies and he'd have to get older to learn about the evil in the world.

One morning, Lucien was by himself and it made him feel older, more responsible even though the grassy vacant lot across the street remained intimidating. Many times, after his mother made him go to bed on Friday nights. He'd go, but wouldn't sleep. He'd lie there, silent, in the dark. He'd hear his older brothers outside on the porch with their friends, talking about the snakes they'd caught over in that same field. Whenever he passed that field, Lucien would always imagine a giant snake rising, rearing its head, opening its mouth, slithering out its tongue and devouring him in one swallow. But the scariest thing of all was getting past the three-story, red-brick abandoned building on the same side of the street where he lived. It looked down upon him with empty, hollow eyes. Overgrown weeds surrounded the front entrance, some so high that a person could stand behind them and not be seen. Some of the brick façade had cracked and fallen to the ground. The neighborhood boys had spent countless hours playing hand grenade, throwing them back up through the few windows that remained. It helped calm him to see the Del Farm supermarket on the other side of the street further down. Lucien sucked in his breath and started to run, quickening his steps and keeping his eyes straight ahead. He bolted and ran past the building and the vacant lot. By now, he was only several doors away from the store.

Inside the store, Joe was stocking the shelves with merchandise when Lucien walked up the concrete step and into the store. A large white deli refrigerator, with a slanting, thick window pane held an assortment of lunch meat, and steak that would be ground into hamburger. Sawdust partially covered the floor, more in some places than others. Lucien stood money in hand, not knowing exactly what to say or do. Joe looked up from his crouching position, wiping the dust off a can of peas and placing it back on the shelf. Joe straightened his tall, slender frame and gave a half smile. His arms showed a tributary of blue-greenish veins that flowed out from his rolled up white shirt sleeves. He saw that Lucien was by himself–only this time, he was without a note from his sister.

"Yes, young man. Can I help you?" Lucien's mouth went dry, so he pointed with his left hand and index finger towards the glass counter casing that held the penny candy. Joe ambled over and stepped behind the counter. "Two for a penny—which do you want?" Joe's wife stood in the doorway, smiling. She craned her neck to see him over the counter. Lucien looked at her and saw a woman whose face held the world. Her eyes, sad and graceful, told Lucien not to be afraid. Her arms, short and somewhat flabby, stuck out from the flowery design on her apron, accenting the short-sleeved dress underneath it.

"Here," Joe said, taking it upon himself to choose for him and placing the candy on the counter. "The Tootsie Rolls are good." He took two of other ones that all the kids called squirrel candy because of the picture on the candy wrapping and placed two on top of the counter. "Four in all," Joe said. "That'll be two cents." Lucien reached up and dropped the nickel on the counter, eying the candy closely. Joe picked up the nickel and reached into an old cigar box with his free hand. His sleeve slid up a little higher on his forearm and Lucien saw the numbers. He thought it was a tattoo. As Joe pulled three pennies out, he noticed that Lucien's attention was on his arm instead of the candy. He quickly lowered his sleeve and looked away. Then he spread the pennies out slowly onto the counter top for Lucien to see. Joe nodded and Lucien grabbed the change. He also grabbed the four pieces of candy. "Thank you," said Lucien. In one motion, Lucien was headed out of the store and onto the sidewalk.

Lucien felt good. He had gone to the store by himself. Bought merchandise and was sure he had gotten the correct change. He would spend the afternoon enjoying his candy and be sure to be back tomorrow.

The next day, Lucien awoke early. No one else was up. The sun boxed with the clouds and tried to push them out of the way. It was an unusually cool morning for summertime. Even without the air-conditioner that his family couldn't afford, the apartment felt cool with the fan in the dining room window still churning. Lucien's plan was to be the first to eat the corn flakes, then, turn on the television to watch the early morning Saturday cartoons. He wasn't as interested as he normally would be. Joe's store and the whole experience from the previous day tested his curiosity and would not let it rest. The numbers on Joe's arm had left an impression and he had made up his mind to ask Joe about them. Lucien wondered whether his wife had them too.

It was going on eight o'clock and he decided to wait no longer. Lucien approached the vacant building with determination and resolve. He would walk, not run past this time. Its towering broken windows looked down and loomed. Lucien gulped and began his uncertain steps past the high weeds at the edge of sidewalk.

"Someone might be hiding there," he had always heard Markus and the other kids say. "Be careful when you pass! Something might jump out and grab you!"

The first blow was the hardest and the deepest—burning, blinding and stinging. His body jerked and weaved like a boxer captured against the ropes by his opponent, unable to defend himself. Lucien gasped for air and tried to balance, but the fists came a second time, glancing off the topside of his forehead. The caved-in staircase led upward on a slant. The broken plaster and glass scratched his backside and arms. He lay motionless, choking back tears. He wrenched his head from side to side to avoid the kisses. His attacker mumbled something through his clenched teeth and hot, sour breath that covered Lucien's brown face.

Then, it was over. Lucien was barely conscious. He lay hurting and shaking uncontrollably on the front walk of the building. When Lucien opened his eyes, he felt the soft, yet strong, firm hands that Joe placed gently underneath him while cradling his battered, bruised head in his arms shushing him in an attempt to quiet Lucien's sobs.

Joe's wife crouched over Lucien, like a nurse tending a soldier wounded in battle. She moaned a song from the old country in a language he didn't understand. She wiped the blood with a white face towel that had turned pink-stained with every motion. She dipped the towel in the warm water in the pan, squeezed it and laid it down.

She shook her head, bit her lip and wiped tears from her own eyes. "Such evil in the world, such evil."

Joe stared at the wall, blinking his black, cavernous eyes searching for an answer. "Yes, and now we both know about it."

Half A Heart

> *Half a heart, girl*
> *Just won't do*
> *Don't want some of your love*
> *Got to have all of you*

The repeated harmony of the last chorus resounded over the P. A. system and the crowd's applause. The Harmonics took its bow in unison. They all walked strutted backstage and fell into a small, crowded dressing room, exhausted and out of breath.

Delaney, the loud-mouthed first tenor, coughed and lit a Kool cigarette. "Damn, Kent! You was blowing too many steps out there!"

Kent looked at Delaney with cold, black, hollow eyes. "Shut up!" he commanded. "Maybe if you stayed on key sometimes, I'd know which way to turn!"

They both feigned violent, forward motions towards each other when Ronald, the bass singer, intervened. "Hey, ladies, knock it off! Okay?" he barked in his best drill sergeant's voice. "We still got one more show to do!"

Delaney slumped back into a beat-up sofa chair, crossed his legs and continued to smoke impatiently. Kent turned away and angrily kicked over a garbage can before opening the door and stepping out into the corridor.

"Where do you think you going, man?" Ronald asked.

Kent squared his shoulders and flexed his neck. "Don't worry bout it. I quit this shit!" Ronald tried to say something in rebuttal, but Kent was already making furious tracks down the hallway for the stage door.

Outside, Kent noticed he had sweated through his stage uniform, a silk, sequined gold and black shirt. Luckily, he also had on his suit jacket. Usually, he'd at least change into a cotton shirt and let the stage shirt dry out before the next show, but the chill of an October evening had already begun to dry the sweat. Kent turned up his high cut collar, reached into his coat pocket and took out a cigarette and lit it. He inhaled slowly and deeply, while the smoke played in his lungs and cooled his nerves. The tar, nicotine and tobacco tore at his throat something fierce. He coughed up phlegm, spat onto the ground. *I'm finished. This is it. No more. I'm just tired.*

Kent wriggled his fifty-eight-year-old body, hunched his shoulders and took another drag. His mind began to wan- der—back to Chicago—back to 1963—back to a simpler, happier time. He gazed up at the silver stars, back grounded by a deep, blue spaciousness. Not a cloud in sight! The Harmonics had been around thirty-five years, which was amazing.

"Man! Thirty-five years," he mused as a half-smile formed his lips. He thought it was amazing, considering the number of R&B groups that had formed in his neighborhood alone. Everybody wanted to sing, even those who couldn't carry a note. The girls on the block loved it. Some groups lasted all of six months—some maybe two weeks.

But for some unearthly reason he, Delaney, Ronald and Roy had started out together at seventeen years of age, made a pact and remained a group. Back then, they were like brothers, closer to each other than their own families. 1963 was an ideal time or so it seemed to them then. A car roaring past and splashing him with the afternoon's rain momentarily brought him back into the present. He cursed the unknown driver as he tried to wipe clean his silk pants.

Kent decided to walk to keep warm. The temperature had dropped ten degrees in the half an hour he had been standing at the mouth of the alleyway. Rounding the corner, he looked up at the marquee hanging in front of the theater. The letters and names looked like the large markings of a child just learning to write. Some of the bulbs had blown out. Some of the letters in the names were missing, but not enough so that one couldn't discern. Fortunately, the theater's management had enough respect and hadn't butchered the group's name. Their manager could still demand thirty to forty minutes of stage time from most promoters. Still, Kent felt that the group had become an oldie but goodie, but because the older ones still remembered their top-ten song "Half A Heart," they always gave them a break. Kent thought it was amazing how one hit could carry a group for years in the business.

He looked at his watch. It was close to 10:00. He began to feel the east coast chill again. He decided to go over to Redman's, the coffee shop across the street and make plans to leave New York on the first thing smoking.

He and the other members of the Harmonics used to live at Redman's years ago. John Redman was the Jew who owned it then. He even had a stake in the theatre. Meals were basically free for any of the talent performing that night. Redman was so cool, he didn't even deduct it from their salary. After he died, his son took over and things changed. Everything had to be accounted for one way or the other. The son didn't let a nickel get past him if he could help it. He had no idea who owned it now and really didn't give a damn. Time had changed everything.

Kent walked with brisk strides towards the facing curb. He rushed through the door. The patrons sat huddled over their coffee cups, rolls and sandwiches in deep concentration. A few glanced at Kent as if he'd interrupted a church service when he'd only let out a little of the heat.

Kent walked quickly and blew warm air into his cupped hands as he headed for the first empty stool at the counter. The waitress did not move. She looked in his direction and waited for a signal. Kent motioned with his head towards the coffee machine. She moved in one swift motion, grabbing a cup and pouring the coffee while half looking at the sweet rolls that sat on the counter a few feet away from him. Kent gave his head motion, communicating in an unspoken silence that made things very comfortable.

The waitress swirled without spilling a drop, reached over with a one-handed motion, removed a chocolate donut and closed the lid. Finally, she sat his coffee and roll in front of him. "$1.35, babe." Kent reached into his pocket, took out his wallet and fished out three dollars. He laid the bills on the scarred counter top and slid them over towards the waitress. The waitress grabbed the money off the counter, and without asking, placed the bills into her pocket. "Need a refill, let me know, okay?"

Kent smiled, "Okay, babe." He poured two creams into his coffee and hoped that after drinking it, his ulcer wouldn't kick up on him. A doctor had warned him fifteen years ago about the caffeine. He took a sip and waited for the pain. Nothing happened.

Maybe I'll actually get to drink a whole cup of coffee today, he thought.

Kent lit another cigarette. He stared blankly at the plates, cups and saucers in the cabinet across from the counter. He wondered whether to take a cab to the bus station. If he got to the station by midnight, he would be back in Chicago by eight the next morning. His decision to leave would be based on a lot of things. The guys in the group whom he once loved and now only tolerated. The growing arthritis in his knees that had once left him doubled up in a fetal position in a dressing room. His growing addiction to the painkillers, laced with steroids. The twenty-two-year-old he had been seeing on the side because all she wanted to do was buy clothes and get her hair done. The broken-down tour bus that would make sure it stopped in the middle of nowhere. The thought of having to iron his own uniform. "Women's work," he called it.

He thought about his wife, Juanita. Married 25 years, she was long suffering and from the old school. They had met at fifteen and still held on to each other. At 52, Juanita was still fine and had kept her shape. The other guys envied him to this day, because she stuck by him even when they didn't have a hit. Many times, over the years, she bore the brunt of the bills when work was scarce. Twenty-five years and six second-mortgages later, she still loved him. The intermittent royalty checks from "Half A Heart" and her nursing salary released the stress and embarrassment.

The group was always on the cusp of national fame and the all-elusive contract with a major label. Motown never came true. A release with an independent label gave the Harmonics neighborhood bragging rights. They had had auditions with the majors, even after the record sold several hundred thousand copies.

Over the years, many times Juanita tried to make it known. "Y'all better get a lawyer. We got bills to pay!"

"Don't worry, baby. Jimmy wouldn't jive me. If it wasn't for us, he wouldn't have a label. Without us, he ain't got nothing."

"Y'all don't even have a contract. How can you trust these people? Yeah, you got a Cadillac out of the deal. But Kent, baby, we can't eat no gasoline!"

Kent could feel himself drowning in a sea of reasons to leave, and he didn't need this anymore. He stirred his coffee and stared at the circles his spoon made. His mind melted into them and he became lost inside a mental time warp.

"Hey, man, let's run through that one more time," said Jimmy, the producer sitting at the control board.

The Harmonics let out a groan in unison as Ronald spoke for the group. "Com'on, man, we done been through this twenty thousand times! When we gon' be finished?"

Jimmy tapped his pen impatiently on the board. "Be cool, man, just be cool. Like I told you guys, this is gonna be a hit song if you just follow my lead!"

They hit again. And nailed it this time. The spirit and the muse had come. Kent's vocal chords opened up to the magic. His honey-sounding tenor embraced the mic and filtered through the speakers. The approving smile on Jimmy's face shined through the glass from the control room as he bobbed his head.

It was a hit and then some. "Half A Heart" went straight through the roof. The fans and the DJs ate it up. American Bandstand, Shindig and anything else the manager could book. City to city, town-to-town, hotel-to-hotel—everything a group could desire. The women, the drugs—everything. While the popularity lasted, the Harmonics enjoyed every bit of it until the well ran dry and the money stopped coming in.

Kent smiled and nodded towards the waitress. "More java." The waitress smiled and looked him over. She knew he was across the the street at the theatre. Then she poured more coffee.

Kent gave it back, smiled again. He rubbed his stomach. She knew why. He played with his thoughts. *Twenty years ago, I'd been on her like white on rice coming in through the door.* But at this stage of the game, he didn't have time for it. Didn't even care.

The noisy crowd of teenagers bursting through the door startled Kent. They headed straight for the jukebox.

"Oh no," he moaned softly to himself. "I don't need to hear that alternative rap crap or whatever they call it nowadays."

But when the music started, Kent was mildly surprised to find himself tapping his foot to the beat. He looked down at his worn-out Stacy Adams. They still had some shine from the afternoon. He also realized the bass line in the song was a reversal of the first four notes to "Half A Heart," sped up to a two-four beat. The singer's screaming didn't sound like anything to write home about, but he could pass.

Lots of reverb, Kent thought. He looked at the young people seated at the far table. *They think they invented everything.* But he knew now that nothing ever really changes. Every generation just finds a different way of saying it.

Kent took a deep breath as he arose from the chair. He went into his pocket and pulled out a dollar and dropped it on the counter. He tipped his invisible hat towards her. She smiled and blew him a kiss.

On the street, Kent walked briskly back towards the theater. He looked at his watch. 10:30 on the dot, fifteen minutes before show time. He quickened his steps crossing the street, almost trotting. The marquee loomed large. With each step, it became larger and larger. His movements were panther-like of the dancer he became on the stage. He turned the corner into the alley. Ronald had left the stage door ajar. Kent smiled again. The spark of leaving had left.

The Harmonics stood, lined up like little fourth graders waiting for the bathroom. Ronald called the roll.

Everybody said, "Yeah!"

Ronald looked at Kent and whispered. "Ready, man?"

Kent brushed off his suit and smoothed the crease in his pants. "Better late than never, baby."

Chasing Rainbows

Bonaparte, Low Boy, Adam and Malik always set out to find the end of the rainbow after a hard rain storm. The faster they ran, the more they tried, the more tired Adam would become. His heavy legs pounded the concrete like a running back breaking tackles five yards away from the goal line. Bone and the others would step up the pace on purpose just to mess with him. The rainbow's colors of red, yellow, blue and orange represented them all. Each would pick a favorite before starting the journey. The streets stretched as far as their innocent eyes could see. The Sears Tower was the end of the world.

"All the way downtown!" Bone shouted.

They rounded the corner of Laverne and Madison and inhaled the aromas rolling out of Joe's Bar-b-que Shack. A mini-tip with mild sauce danced in their heads. The years moved like slow motion. The days were full of snowball syrups, hot dogs, basketball games and harassing the Arab store owners. The streets had not yet stolen their innocence.

* * *

The night's evening came as it always did, sounds of lonely

moans, idle talk, whoops, hollers and phone calls. Bone saw that Adam never lined up next to the pay phones like everyone else. He wondered whether Adam knew any numbers or even how to make a call. Adam's mother would come sometimes and sit with him in the visitor's room. Bone would sit nearby with his mother and grandma, half-listening to the conversation. It was always a one-sided monologue, Adam's mother mouthing words through her tears and stringy, blonde-streaked hair. Adam sat in a motionless somber, nodding his head every now and then as if he understood. There were days when Adam's aunt would come with her. Bone never saw any other children besides Adam's two sisters.

Bone lay on his bunk and stared at the ceiling, his breaths coming slow and measured. He heard Adam's low snoring through the cell block noise, while he contemplated his return to the block. When he got back on the block, he would do something different, but he didn't know exactly what. But this street thing had to change. The last conversation with his public defender had him ranting and roiling his mind.

"Look mam'. I'm going up, down or out. Ain't no other way around it. I know I still got my uncles, but they ain't me and I ain't them. I can't let those streets claim me. It's not gonna be my fate!"

The same fate that had not yet claimed him, stalked him closely. Bone smiled to himself and brushed the mustache he had struggled to grow since he was 17 years old in Mr. Miller's literature class. He remembered how the words *fate and irony* had come up one time in a literature class discussion. When Mr. Miller gave the definitions, Bone sat up in his chair, cleared his ears and shook off the blunt's haze smoked earlier that morning. The main character of the story the class read was *caught up* as

Bone would put it. He saw himself like the character, trying to wrangle his way out of another situation, and like Bone's life, seeing it end with a turn of bad luck.

Bone thought of Jimmy, one of the older brothers on the block who had put his hoop skills to use and played semipro and came back home. They'd stand, leaning on the fence in front of Marcy Center. Bone leaned forward and looked down a corridor of sun blinking through green leaves and rushing birds to 15th and Springfield. Jimmy now worked as a group worker at the center, the same place where Bone had spent his daycare years while his mother and grandmother were at work. Every time Jimmy managed to engage Bone in a conversation, he left Bone with a hint of wisdom before going back inside the center. *Man, thirty seconds in the other direction, that's me!* Bone knew exactly what Jimmy was talking about.

* * *

Adam's grunts and the sound of water on water brought him back. Bone was so deep into thought that he hadn't noticed that Adam had awoken, gotten out of his bunk and was standing at the toilet with his back to him. Bone turned over, pretending that he didn't see—though years ago, he got curious about what got those girls' panties into such a frenzy at the alternative high school. Adam finished and plodded back over to his bunk and lay down. Within minutes he was sleep again, snoring and grunting. The dream must be good.

Bone longed for a Newport. He could taste it. See it. Smell it. Feel it between his fingers. The ban by the Cook County sheriff's office had helped some inmates kick the habit. Bone thought there should be designated smoking areas somewhere. A cold forty wouldn't be bad either. His uncles would laugh at him and his buddies when they'd come to his grandma's bar-b-ques in the summertime. Then, they would plunge into stories about back in the day, when the only beer their parents drank was Budweiser.

"Aw man! Budweiser? Whoooo shit!"

"Better than that mess y'all drinking," his uncles sang in unison. Then somewhere in between, Bone's grandma would cool down the conflict.

Somehow, Bone had to get Adam to talk. As long as he'd known him, Adam had never said much. Bone couldn't even remember the sound of his autistic voice. Bone and Malik mulled Adam's future.

"Man, I don't mind protecting him, but at least he should show some gratitude." Bone shuffled his feet and leaned back in his chair.

Malik wrinkled his forehead and rubbed his beard. He knew that Adam needed to figure out how to show gratitude. "Man, I know you ain't looking for gratitude like that; I know you don't roll like that, but I understand. We gots to keep an eye on Lovelace and his girls though. Heard they had Adam surrounded in the shower while the guards looked the other way. They don't give a damn."

"Yep. Had him until I threw my uncles' names out at 'em. Those guards moved like a slave with a burning match under his ass. I know they thought I was crazy. Lovelace and his niggers recognized and backed off."

Adam had become a walking enigma. The special education track Adam's mother pulled him out of could have done him a lot of good, but she didn't want him to feel different. By the time Adam had been socially passed through tenth grade, it was too late. Adam had turned eighteen, his teachers had given up on him and a last ditch effort by his mama led to an alternative program. A lot of students like Adam and Bone turned to it when the regular system failed. Two teachers at the alternative, Mr. Miller and Ms. Howard, didn't know that Adam would grab their hearts and steal them away like a hurricane does a roof.

Working with Adam was an adventure from one day to the next. Ms. Howard would look at him and shake her head, roll her eyes and muffle a laugh that spit pity. Mr. Miller would do the same before gently telling Adam that it was time to go to the next class. His eyes whispered *help me.* They did what they could. Every movement was another step up the mountain. It could be Adam's clothes. It could be his shoes. It could be his hair. He'd always try to fit in with the other students. His dark chocolate skin was smooth, except for a few discolored spots on his forehead. He wore overalls and oversized white T's. He carried a book bag filled with words he would never understand. Adam's skin would be swathed in grease and glistened in the winter months. The girls in the room would whisper. Finally, one would come up and ask Mr. Miller if they could take Adam to the bathroom and help fix him up. What else they did in the bathroom, Miller never asked.

After they explained to him that it was time to change classes, Adam rose with his mighty, two-hundred-pound torso and ambled down the hall. The time and special attention Ms. Howard and Mr. Miller gave Adam made him feel special around the other students. They just couldn't understand why he warranted it. In class, they would be extra careful not to call on him. They knew he didn't know the answer. They'd always tell him to keep trying, but time after time, it was the same old test scores. *Why did the gods do this to you? Why you?* Miller and

Howard thought Adam's mother must have asked herself that question a million times.

* * *

The court room was not crowded like it usually was on Mondays. The judges like to hold court on Mondays, Bone thought. Bone saw his mother and grandma. He saw Adam's mother and aunt too. Bone's public defender sat at the table, shuffling papers and looking at her watch. She probably had ten other cases to defend that day. They had talked two weeks ago. She concluded that the drugs were planted on Bone and that she would emphasize that in his defense. She would base it on the fact that Bone had prior contact with the arresting officers earlier that year when they raided the *50 Yard Line Club*. Almost everybody they busted that night caught a case except Bone and several other people. But they knew Bone was living dirty, trying to make a living. Not that they hadn't seen it before, but what pissed them off was that Bone was being arrogant about it, bragging up and down the block that they couldn't touch him because he was protected.

The courtroom was humming silence when Adam entered. He still had the same blank look on his face, though his hair was shorter. Adam always had battles with his hair and the stress of being a prisoner made it start to fall out. Lighting struck when Adam waddled over to the table, shackled like a slave. He squinted his eyes. The judge looked like a giant monster in a robe. Adam hadn't made heads or tails out of anything that had been said by the bailiff or the attorneys. Adam had a private attorney. Two young brothers who were dressed professionally and looked like they knew what they were doing. Three weeks earlier, they had called Mr. Miller and asked him to come in as a witness for Adam. They wanted Miller to testify that Adam's mental capabilities were deficient and he didn't understand when the police read him his rights. The prosecutor asked the judge if he could treat Miller as a hostile witness since he didn't know that he was coming to testify. The judge granted permission.

Miller was called in while he waited on the other side of the slanted, smoked glass with Adam's mother and his aunt. Miller sat in the witness and tried not to look directly at Adam. It was hard. Miller looked at Adam's mother and remembered meeting her at the school, but he had never met the aunt and it became clear where Adam got his broad shoulders, big chest, large forearms and wide rump. The prosecutor began questioning his hostile witness and it showed that he was a little flummoxed, and angry that he didn't know Miller was coming. No matter what he asked Miller, he could not trip him up. Miller explained that Adam would have never understood the instructions of the Miranda rights read by the arresting officers. As evidence, he explained that the basic skills test scores were on file at the school as proof of Adam's reasoning and critical thinking skills. Adam's attorneys had no questions, so the judge excused Miller.

By the time Miller got to the door, Adam's mother and aunt were also leaving. One of the attorneys followed closely. Out in the hall, the attorney praised Miller for his sharp, clear answers.

"This should really help us out. Cause, y'know, in these kinds of cases, the judge can really be hard. And when the state moves in, it doesn't help."

"How hard can he be on an auto theft case?" Miller rubbed his curious chin.

"Auto theft? Wait... didn't you know?"

"You guys told me over the phone that's what it was."

Miller turned towards Adam's mother, then the attorney

spilled the beans all over the floor. "Wow! This is a molestation case... his two little cousins?" He nodded towards the aunt. "She tried not to press charges, but somehow the DCFS got wind of it and the state moved in. Man, I thought you knew."

Miller reached out for the wall to steady himself. He wasn't prepared to hear that shit. He swung around and leaned, leaving sweaty hand prints before pushing himself upright. He gave Adam's mother a confused dirty look, turned and made tracks to the elevator. Nothing in Miller's head sat right. The sweat made its way down the spine of his back and underneath his armpits. What would he tell Ms. Howard? What would he tell his other coworkers? Outside, the cool spring air dried his face. He felt like he had been sucker punched in the gut. His pain was not for himself. It was for Adam and all the other Adams in the world. 26th and California and its tombs held a welcome mat.

They got a continuance for Adam.

* * *

Bone jumped down from his bed and did some pushups. Then he did some sit-ups, stretched his legs, grabbing his toes and leaning forward. He thought about his mother. He thought about his grandma. He thought about how his grandma would sit him on her lap when he was little and weave the story of how he got such a funny name for a brother. He had always wondered why his mama give him such a funny name like Bonaparte. *Adam should have this name,* he thought. The story his grandma gave him one day he came home from school never left. He was in second grade and the innocent cruelty of kids reared its head and his classmates were teasing the hell out of him. Bone ran home and fell into grandma's lap. She messaged his head and twirled his locs.

"What's wrong with you, boy? Why you crying so?" She knew this day was coming and that she would have to explain. Her daughter wouldn't know how.

"Grandma, them boys... them boys at school..." Bone could hardly catch his breath.

"What? They say something 'bout your name? That's it, isn't it?" She handed Bone a tissue. "Well, let me tell you the story 'bout how you got that name. See, there was a time you didn't have no name. Your mama and you was still at the hospital and she hadn't named you yet."

"You mean I didn't have no name at all?"

"Oh, you had a name, a last name. Jameson, just like me."

"So, how'd I get my first name?"

"Long before me and your mama was born somebody named you."

"Who? Grandma, who?"

"See, son, when I was still down in Louisiana, my grandma had married a Frenchman. And his last name was Bonaparte. He was white. They had children, what they called mixed."

"Mixed with what?"

"Black and white, silly."

"Oh."

"Well, they children had children and so forth and soon... when my grandma and her husband was still living, they caught hell every which way for being together. So they split. But before they split, he made her promise that she'd keep his name, or one of the kids born down the line would. She promised, but went on to remarry a Jameson. Years and years passed of everybody avoiding naming they child after a Bonaparte because nobody on that side of the family ever accepted us anyway. Well, leave it to me to get tired of all that mess that night in the hospital. And that's how you got your name. You a special child. I wonder what that no good family would think of us now. I guess they thought when we left the south, we left the name."

By the time Grandma finished, Bone was well into his after-noon nap.

* * *

The cafeteria was loud and full. Adam ate his food like a pig, never stopping to slow down. Just shoveling the food into his mouth like it was his last meal. Some of the dudes teased him trying to get him to take a spoonful. Lovelace and his girls egged him on. After he finished, he just sat and stared straight ahead waiting for the guards to say that breakfast was over. Malik's situation was better off, because he was Muslim and didn't hesitate to let it be known. From the way he walked, the way he interacted with the guards and the way the guards reacted to him said it all as soon as he stepped in the joint.

Malik would hold court in the recreation area on Friday evenings, spitting philosophy and explaining the white world. "I know why I'm here. Do you?" Malik licked his lips because he knew he had distracted his opponent.

"Huh? What?" The inmate was confused and tried to redirect his attention back to the board.

"They still trying to catch up with my brother. Can't find him. They don't know if he's in Cali or Chicago." His brother had gotten away in a drug deal gone bad. The FBI was still looking for him. No matter how they threatened, Malik wouldn't turn over on him. Malik had resigned himself to do the time and not let it do him. Fifteen years was no joke. "Checkmate!" Malik said, looking for who was next up.

Malik's game was chess. Bone was one of a few who could challenge him. Their game went back to the eighth grade before they all started to grow into separate ways. They liked dazzling the young and the old inmates. Malik would often say that the board was spiritual Not even the guards would touch the holy grail. When the other inmates would gather around, Malik would use the opportunity to hold court and spit some knowledge. Bone always knew when he was going to launch into one of his sermons. Malik's hawk-like eyes would grow narrow and pierce the air like he was looking for the smallest speck of dust on the floor. Malik kept the Koran at the side of his bed and prayed five times a day without fail.

"If you only you would cross over, man. We could rule the world." Even though Malik meant every word, Bone knew he was also trying throw him off of his game. "Common everyday people just don't know."

"Don't know what?"

"You know... the word," Malik said, planning his next move.

"What word? What's the word?" Bone moved his knight.

"Reparations, my brother. Reparations!" Then, Malik would smile as he made a move with his knight as well. They both agreed that the knight was the baddest piece on the board. Even badder than the king and the queen. Once he started, Malik wouldn't stop, "Can't nobody move like the knight. Somebody always trying to checkmate the king or take out the queen. They always relying on somebody to protect them. But the knight is so bad that it protects itself. Somebody gets too close, he'll hit 'em like L-Seven. And you can use the knight to set up all kinds of shit. Nobody ever sees it coming. Then bam! There goes the knight from the backside swooping in."

To them, the knight was the truth.

"What about God?" At times, Malik would broach the subject with Bone. With Adam, it was useless. "Well, is God and Allah the same?" Bone stared at Malik between moves and reared back in his chair and stretched his legs.

Undaunted, Malik scratched his chin. "Yeah. Didn't you know?"

"Why ain't they got the same name, then?"

"Cause. They didn't come from the same people. One people said he had no name; the other people called him Allah. So, I just call him God-Allah."

"Hmmm..."

"That's so I don't get Moms so upset and she starts grabbing her chest and having asthma attacks and shit. It was bad enough that the two youngest children started praying five times a day and reading *that book* as she calls it. It's like the difference between jazz and R&B." Malik smiled.

Bone smiled too. "Yeah, right."

Bone's grandma made sure that he got a dose of old time religion as a child. She knew she couldn't rely on his mama to give it to him. The First Church of Deliverance was Grandma's home and had been for the last forty years. Every Sunday and most Wednesdays, without fail, she would take Bone to services. His young mind would marvel at the preacher, the shouting, the prayers and the Holy Ghost. It kept his mind off of friends. He knew were out in the streets playing like kids do. Bone's Sunday school teacher was happy for him and made it known that he was extremely pleased with his reading skills. Every time he needed someone to read verse, he would ask the class, then eye Bone and give him his cue. Bone liked the acknowledgement. The only thing the teacher didn't like was when Bone would get a head of steam after his reading and start asking questions he didn't think a ten-year-old should ask. *Where did God come from? Who left him in charge? And if He was in charge, how did He let things get out of hand like this? Why didn't He just kick the devil's ass and send him on his way?* Bone would calm down when the superintendent would threaten to beat the devil out of him as if he was his child, but in the end, would only tell his grandma on him.

The class laughed and the superintendent lost control. He approached Bone's grandma. "Sister, with all due respect, I think you should speak to your grandson. His behavior is... well, it's not what it should be. Maybe it's from being around his uncles... if you know what I mean..."

But Grandma would defend Bone and tell the superintendent that those were her children and she would decide when and how much Bone would see them. "And, furthermo', the boy's just askin' questions—why don't you answer 'em?"

The superintendent would grab his bible and storm into the sanctuary.

* * *

The prosecutors and Bone's attorney were worn out from unrealistic caseloads. They just wanted to get this thing over with. But one of the prosecutors was determined to do his job and that was to not let Bone back out on the street without sending him a message. A message that said if you choose to keep living like you're living, we're going to lock you up and throw away the key. Literally.

"There's not a lot he can do out there," Bone's mouthpiece protested. "His choices are limited. You know that."

"Limited? What's limiting about attending school and work at a job? He's been in and out of the system for the last eight years."

"And who's fault is that?" Bone's attorney reached at the straws that hung in the air.

The prosecutor would not let up. "Fault? Wanna talk about fault? Let's lay it where it should really go. These guys run around like it's the wild wild west out there, doing whatever they feel without regards for anybody. Not even themselves." He banged an open hand on the table for emphasis.

"Those cops harassed this boy!"

"He's a man, not a boy."

"You know and I know that we've been throwing these teens down state with adults as soon as they turn 18. Maybe even sooner."

The state's attorney slumped back in his chair and shook his head from side to side. He knew that he was not going to win this battle. He was just too tired to argue. Tomorrow, there would be another just like this one. "Alright. We'll look at what he's done so far and consider—just *consider*—parole."

Bone's attorney smiled, grabbed her files and practically ran out of the room before he changed his mind.

* * *

Low Boy had caught a bad break. Bone didn't think it was so bad though. The judge forced them to take him out of general population and put him into a special population. So now he didn't have to deal with all the other bullshit. Low Boy was in the infirmary after they had brought him back from the Stroger Hospital. Bone made a point to try and get a detail in the infirmary. He succeeded and promised to bring a report to Malik, just in case they weren't treating Low Boy right.

"How they treating you, man?"

Low Boy pushed himself up on his elbow to face Bone. He fell into his Black Puerto Rican speak. "I'm okay. Abracadabra. Sis boom bah. Everything still works, man." Low Boy grabbed his crotch underneath the sheet and managed a smile.

Bone reached out his fist for some dap and Low Boy accommodated. Two years earlier, Low Boy tried to stick up a cell phone store. He succeeded until the clerk pulled out a gun and shot him in the back as he ran out of the door. The bullet was so close to the spine, the doctors decided not to try to take it out, but the bullet started to poison Low Boy's system.

Low Boy laid back down and stared at the ceiling. "What's up with Adam?"

"You know, well, Adam... he'll be alright. They know I gots my finger on him."

"Malik?"

"Man, you know Malik. He can take care of hisself."

"What you gon' do when you get out, man?"

"I don't know, man. But I'm gon' do something. My granny say I can stay with her, but I gots to work, y'know? Moms... well, I don't want to talk about Moms..."

Low Boy let out a sigh and closed his eyes. Bone took the hint and got up, grabbed his mop and left.

* * *

The guard gave Bone an envelope. "See you on the next go round, man."

"Shit. I ain't coming back here. That's for sho', brother."

Bone turned and walked through the gates. They closed behind him with a sound that rattled his brain. Bone stood on 26th and California Streets waiting on the bus. He pulled his collar up over his neck. The Chicago hawk was breathing again, but he was glad to feel it. Damn glad. Then, it hit him: he remembered the sound of Adam's voice.

One of those mornings after a storm when they were chasing the rainbow and running down Madison Street, Adam blurted out: "how come it ain't no black in the rainbow?"

Redemption

This is a story about the trinity and its redemption, if there is any. It just must be told. Maybe my telling will make people understand better. Maybe it won't. Maybe it won't change the way the world looks at Black boys. I'll say this though: it won't change the fact that they are killed in a cold, cruel way.

It started the day I went to check out a killing in Douglas Park. It was late summer. The streets were full of lulls and slow life movements. The boy, or as Trinity would call him—the man child—was found lifeless under the viaduct near the grass. When we spoke on the phone, Trinity's reporter's instincts told him there was more to the story than Sergeant Bryant and the department would let on and that I should press him on it. Even the superintendent showed up and looked around. He was probably scared that there might be a riot because everyone in the neighborhood knew the boy.

When I got there, I spied the superintendent slither into his waiting police car surrounded by his bodyguards and pull away. He was sure gonna need them if the community didn't hear the answers it was looking for. He probably suspected that the Panthers had something to do with it. The Panthers run breakfast programs for our kids—why would they kill Black teenagers? Just wouldn't make sense. Underneath the viaduct, where he lay, I couldn't get a clear view because of the crowd, so I decided to push my way through to Sergeant Bryant. The whole scene felt weird. Bryant's brow furrowed a worried look. When I looked at the boy, I could see why. I had a feeling that the placement of the body was staged, like somebody had laid him there instead of his just collapsing.

"Can I ask you a question, Sarge?"

Worry spoke. "How in the hell did you get over here? Y'know I ought to have you arrested!"

"There's something else going on ain't it, Sarge?" I leaned forward meeting him eye to eye.

He raised his hand telling me to keep my voice down. "Look, Gina, don't go starting something that isn't on fire. It's too hot and too tense already. But I know you're going to write what you want."

"Just let me ask: is this connected to the last one?" I kept fishing to see if he'd let his guard down, but he wouldn't take that bait. He summoned over two officers like he always did when he couldn't talk.

Sergeant Bryant knew my father. They had been running buddies at Roosevelt University back in the 1950's. When he could, Sarge would feed me information that other journalists would get later in an official police report. Sarge was a WWII veteran and had a military style just like my boss at Betts. He knew and lived by the rules. That's why they made him a sergeant. But, he always had a soft spot for the young black males in Lawndale. He knew well the forces they were up against, yet also knew that they could get themselves in a pile of shit just by being stupid. He knew the kind of forces that made young boys pimp with a lean and stiff-legged walk. And also the kind that crushed a burgeoning manhood after seeing a drunk father on the holidays, leaving a mother and his frustrations on her ass on the kitchen floor. The kind that spring up out of the bushes and try to stop him from standing how a man is supposed to stand and not bent over so people can ride him home.

Like Father, after Sarge would feed me info, he'd give his lecture about not using it to make him look bad. I think the other sergeants suspected this was going on, but couldn't prove it. Sarge still thought I didn't know he was keeping tabs on me for Father. Ever since we fell out about my leaving Spelman, killing *his* dream and moving into Lawndale to take a job with Betts, Father and I didn't talk—we argued, mainly about Black folks' problems and solutions.

Father is a staunch Republican; his father was a Republican and his grandfather worshipped the ground Lincoln walked on during Reconstruction. They had pledged their lives to the party and so did Father. Booker T. Washington was the end-all. Father couldn't stand what he assumed to be the laziness of Boor blacks and always preached of their refusal to "cast down the bucket and pull themselves up by the bootstraps." Sarge was a Republican too, but the sociology classes at Roosevelt also told him that institutional racism still determined some things and law enforcement was one of them. That was the only place Sarge and Father differed. The rest was personal responsibility all the way.

I knew that Sarge would go back to his office and get on the phone telling Father that I needed to back off this case because the superintendent was turning up the screws and that the public didn't need to know everything right now. He'd ask if he could he talk to me and settle me down. Sarge had done this before. Father would send a message through Mother. Mother would call, I'd say yes and hang up because I knew why she was calling. I'd see Father sitting at his oak wood desk laughing and Mother running into his office asking what he thought was so funny about their daughter hanging up on her like that. Father would say nothing and smile his wickedest smile.

"This reporter is out of bounds," Sarge said. "Put her back behind the lines!" I didn't wait for the officers. I closed my notebook and turned, quick-stepping back into the crowd.

The people milled in the August heat, standing in the soaked streets. I listened to the conversations going back and forth from one bystander to the next. Their voices melded into a chorus of warnings and prayers calling on the angels that hovered above the boy's body. *"That's old man's Beckham's grandson. Man, his Mama's gon' be sick!"*

It was close to noon and already burning up. I sat in my car, smelling the stench rise from the overnight garbage in the street. I thought about the family's name, Beckham. Trinity probably knew them. I thought about the boy's mother.

I decided to head back to the office. Lunch time was almost over. The last thing I needed was Jonas' bitching about how he didn't pay me to run around the city chasing a story that didn't pan out. I knew he was poking his head out of his office every fifteen minutes bugging our secretary Margret about where I was and when was I coming back. My editor Jonas was more bark than bite, a total cliché if there ever was one. He was a former Marine whose pants' crease still walked the line. His stride from one office to the next never changed. He was always on a mission to destroy. He refused the afro, still wearing a close-cropped cut with clipped side burns. Whenever he was out of the office, Trinity and I joked about whether or not he was still fighting World War II.

I lit a Kool and started the car, pulling into the street. I watched the crowd through the rearview mirror and drove down Douglas Boulevard. I didn't have to turn on the radio. Somebody always either had a speaker in the window or a radio sitting on a bench blaring the pleas of Al Green, telling us to somehow stay together. I understood why. The community had splintered something fierce after 1969 and I hated that. Even the Panthers had been effectively shut down by the Hoover boys, and it seemed like everywhere you looked there was some poverty program attached to some poverty money. Just like the store front churches that smothered 16th Street. Everybody singing and shouting for the same things, but couldn't agree on how to get to heaven. Seemed like the only person who had some sense to me was Curtis Mayfield and nobody stopped to hear what he was saying. I knew people got thrown into a whirlwind of things sometimes. You can grab on to the nearest rope and an invisible hand always seems to be trying to pull you off. But that's when the old folks say you hang on for dear life and sing the blues to get you through the night terrors.

After the morgue truck had taken the body, the crowd still refused to leave.

* * *

At the office, I placed a couple of calls to the Beckham family. I didn't get an answer. My mind was distracted. Mostly, I thought on Trinity and his family. I knew he was always trying to keep tabs on Lynn. She was still having a hard time. Lynn's life had taken her into the underworld, full blast. One time, Trinity got a frantic call from his Mama telling him that Lynn's best friend had called and said somebody needed to go see about her. Trinity knew the streets of Lawndale and the first place he headed was Andrew's basement on 13th and Millard around the corner from Stone Temple Baptist Church.

Andrew's basement was where all the hypes could relax and cure their ills and nod. The basement was lit by candles. Two legless couches faced the door. Behind the couches was a poster of Uncle Sam pointing his wrinkled finger at everyone who dared enter. This was apropos for Andrew, having done his stint in Nam and coming back into the world with the monkey riding him hard into the madness of urban warfare. Two dingy white throw rugs laid on what was left of the linoleum, worn away to the concrete. A coffee table, with spent syringes and burnt spoons. A white sheet, spattered with blood draped it. One door, leading to a bedroom, was always closed. Andrew sat in a large, high-back straw chair when he presided, stirring his unholy mayhem. The stench of death hung in a brew of unwashed bodies.

Trinity pulled up to Andrew's house. A short walk and silent prayer tried to cool his nerves. He started through the fence, but was stopped in his tracks. A man named Funkee, about the same age as Lynn, stood staggering, leaning on an invisible prop. He sniffed and rubbed his nose, trying to straighten up, never reaching a full tilt.

"Look, man, I'm just here for my family—know what I mean?" Trinity said.

"I know, but you late man." Trinity stiffened, preparing for the worse. "Man, they went to Cook County two hours ago. They got a pulse, but that was some mean shit she took."

"The County, huh?"

"Yeah, baby. Yeah."

Look, man. I gots to go, know what I mean?"

"Man, you gon' leave a brother hangin'? I could a told you

anything." Funkee grabbed his crotch and hunched.

"Told me anything? Man, you must be crazy! What are you gonna tell me that's gonna make me listen?"

"The man in blue—baby blue, baby blu-ue..." Funkee sang in a cryptic nursery rhyme and laughed.

"The blue what? Boy, that shit has completely blown your mind." Trinity waved him off. He was going to see about Lynn.

Funkee danced and continued to sing as Trinity drove away. *"The man in blue—the man in blue."*

* * *

Cook County's triage was an organized chaos. There was no other place like it in Chicago. When the residents did their training in the County's ER and survived, they could withstand anything in anybody's hospital. Trinity entered through the north end façade where an early 19th century architecture stood guard. He and Lynn had been born there. Lack of health insurance at Betts still had him using the County's Fantus Clinic for what ailed him. Father always paid for me to see a private doctor.

Trinity quickened his steps and headed for the information desk to get a visitor's pass. He made his way down the hall to the ER, where a nurse stood frowning with her hands on her hips.

"Yes, can I help you?" she asked, brushing her hair and fanning with a clipboard.

"Evelyn Stevens. Is she here? I think she came in a couple of hours ago."

The nurse ran her index finger down the clipboard. "Are you family?" Trinity went for his wallet, but she waved him off. "She was here, but now she's in a room upstairs. The doctors stabilized her and got her heart going again. Room 910." She flipped him a visitors pass. Then, she looked past Trinity towards the other patients. Trinity got the message and stepped aside. The nurse disappeared into a sea of white coats and uniforms.

Trinity wasted no time getting to an elevator. The door opened to a nurse's station. Trinity flashed his pass as he rushed down the hall to Lynn, but took a deep pause before entering the room. He saw Lynn lying there with an IV running from her forearm into a machine that made a beeping, clicking sound and a hose that sat in her mouth. Trinity breathed easier when he saw that the green lines staggered like graphs on a standardized test. Every now and then he'd hear gurgling sounds like a drain clearing after plunging.

One of the doctors tiptoed into the room. "It's not as bad as it looks. Just pulling the fluid off her lungs. We're being careful with the antibiotics, considering what she already had in her system."

Relieved, Trinity sat down in the chair beside the bed and watched Lynn's chest move up and down in deep, slow movements underneath the white sheets. "Thanks, Doc."

"We'll give it another few days, then, she can go home. Gotta run." The doctor spun through the door and disappeared into the hallway.

Trinity knew exactly what the doctor meant—*already in her system*. In his mind, he spoke softly to Lynn, rubbed her hand and stared at the floor thinking about how their lives had been much simpler growing up. Just him, Lynn and Mama after Daddy died.

Mamas were always left to bear the burdens. Left to see us born into time, one foot here and the other in eternity. Mamas know, as much as it hurts, that children will spend the rest of their lives trying to get back into eternity. Trinity's Mama knew this well. She knew it from her childhood in Mississippi watching her father hitch his mule and sharecropping dreams to a log and a mule that would circle a tree, turning sap into syrup. She knew it when she saw him hunt squirrels that could not escape the eye of his shotgun.

The trees moaned and turned into lightning. The morning service had just let out. The woods in back of the building called the children while the sun glared, bugs clicked and the winds swirled all at once. The congregation knew that the preacher had preached, because the weather changed when they came outside. The old folks would say *the preacher preached so good, it made God stir His soup.* See, if he could make God stir His soup, the trees called, and the lightning answered. The tree split, showing its golden flesh. "The soup must have been good that day," because sparks flared and snaked and found Mama's leg, blew her wet body into the air and into God's palm, leaving three brown spots on her calf for life.

Trinity missed how Mama would pretend to be mad when she came home from work and they hadn't cleaned up. Or the red colored mashed potatoes surprise Lynn tried to cook one day. Mama tried hard to look mad, then burst out laughing so hard the wig on her head shook. At least they still had the pork chops Mama had left in the oven before leaving for work. Trinity and Lynn would sit for hours at the dining room table, reading the Sunday comics. This was where Lynn taught him to read and think. Lynn would read a section and pick out the words she felt he needed to know and make him write them down in a notebook. All these years later, Trinity still had the notebooks neatly stacked in a footlocker at his apartment.

Trinity came out of his revelry, stood up and headed for the door. Tomorrow, he'd bring Mama and Malik to see her. Walking down the hall, he whispered silent prayers again.

* * *

Trinity meant a lot to me. He was the man who stole my heart. No man had ever been able to live up to Father's intelligence besides Trinity. He had always looked after his family. He never had the finances I had coming up. Father kept an insurance office on 16th and Roosevelt Road—money made that he used to move us out of Lawndale in 1965 and into Maywood to live more upscale. Grass replaced the concrete, vacant lots and broken glass. Quiet replaced the evening ambulance sirens. The same people Father called niggers spared his office, because it was black owned during the riots in 1968.

Trinity had always lived on the Westside. 15th and Springfield. 16th and Pulaski. Douglas and Central Park. All over. I remember Trinity telling me about how he got his name.

"I was a breach birth. Nineteen hours of labor just about killed Mama."

He had me then. Trinity saw my wonderment in my eyes. "What did she do?"

"Who? Mama? She just kept asking for Reverend Harris. You know, Daddy was a skeptic. But the thought of losing a wife and son scared the shit out of him and he left the hospital and went to summon him. Mama said Reverend Harris prayed so hard that even Daddy took his hat off."

"So, where did your name come from?"

"See, Mama always believed that it was the Father, Son and Holy Ghost that brought us through. She vowed to name me

144

Trinity. Daddy didn't take it too kindly and told her it didn't make no sense. But Mama remained steadfast and believed that I would be protected for the rest of my life."

* * *

Trinity's responsibilities became huge, especially when Lynn's mind became so frazzled and left Malik to Mama's care. It was two hours after they missed Lynn's leaving the hospital. Mama stood at the kitchen stove, nursing her greens and roast beef. Malik sat glued to *The Three Stooges*' antics on the black and white. A sudden rumbling on the back stairs made Mama reach for the butcher knife on the table. Mama was always ready. Prior happenings with Lynn's friends made her be extra careful.

"Who is it?" Mama said, summoning Jesus and whoever else was listening.

A sandpapered voice answered. "It's me."

"Me who?" she asked, twirling the blade in her hand.

"Me, Mama. Me!"

Mama recognized Lynn's voice, started to place the knife on the table, but slid it into her apron pocket and undid the locks. The door creaked and Lynn lurched into the kitchen. Her red, green and black beret, fatigue jacket and blue jeans were crumpled but clean. A worn copy of *Soul on Ice* hung from her jacket pocket. The hospital wristband still held its place.

"Hey, Mama. What's going on? Heard y'all been looking for me. Well, here I am." Lynn did a two-step and opened her arms for Malik, who stood peering at the kitchen doorway. "Hey, Lil' man. How you doing? Miss me?" Mama blocked Malik's movement towards Lynn, then relented. "Com'on, miss me just a little?" Malik bolted and Lynn bent down to hug him, catching a whiff of the hospital's scent.

"Lord…" Mama sighed, moving to a chair.

"What y'all got to eat?" Lynn asked before Mama could utter another word. Her words were unsteady but truthful.

Mama smoothed her apron over her lap and motioned for Lynn to sit down. "You know you can always eat here. We was at the County, but…"

"I know, I was gone." Lynn lowered herself into the chair, keeping one arm around Malik's shoulder for balance. "I mean the doctors said it was okay."

Nervousness weighed the room, but Malik broke the silence. "Mama, you gon' stay here now?" he asked, crossing his fingers behind his back. Malik had the charm and smile of his father.

The pictures on the mantle in the living room showed Lynn and Sam and a newborn Malik nestled between matching dashikis. Lynn beamed, unaware that Sam's bad heart would take him away from her and Malik nine months later. Even in her life's haze, Lynn could see Sam's fiery intelligence growing in Malik with his reddish-brown mane and high forehead that held all the world's knowledge. It was Sam's precise mind that attracted her to him.

Seems like every time I try to love somebody, they come and take 'em away, she thought to herself. Lynn wanted Sam forever and clung to him like a little girl clutching a teddy bear. And just like that Sam was gone. Malik was here and Sam was gone.

Before he left, Sam had made sure to bless Malik with the blues, so that he could give love and take love, carry drums and set tempos and lead choruses, sail ships and wear chains, scheme science and build erectus, burn fires and collect dust, blow horns and walk streets and chant power. Lynn stroked Malik's head and admired his hair. Yes, he was Sam's progeny.

She teared up and searched for a tissue.

"Mama, don't cry. Why are you crying?"

"I'm just happy for you, baby, that's all." Lynn wiped her cheeks, reached for a fork and plunged into the roast beef and greens Mama had placed in front of her. Mama shot worried glances at Lynn and bowed her head in solace at the memory of the young girl who had grown into a woman she did not know anymore.

* * *

Since the Beckhams hadn't answered my phone calls, I decided to take a chance and drop by and see if I could talk to Miss Beckham. The boy's family lived on 16th Street, just off Pulaski Road in a two-story grey-shingled frame. A long wooden staircase ran up to the second floor. When I pulled up, I saw several small children playing in the dirt and grass in the front yard. A fan sat churning in the window of the garden apartment. I got out and approached the fence, fishing my purse for peppermints. The kids sensed it right away. Old Man Beckham sat on the porch at the top of the stairs, listening to Jackie Wilson's shouts of fever on a portable radio. He seemed oblivious to me or was at least pretending while he tapped his brown cane on the battleship grey porch floor. His wide-brimmed hat sheltered him from the sun. A glass of lemonade sweated nearby on a small table.

Leaning forward, he adjusted his glasses, squinted his eyes and clasped his long sunbaked fingers. "Help you, young lady?" He was gruff, direct and suspicious. My eyes darted to the Crisco can sitting next to him. I knew he was dipping snuff. My grandfather had done the same thing whenever his visited us. Father hated his father-in-law's habit and tried to keep the dipping on the back porch, but Mother would let him dip wherever he wanted as long as he kept the can. I loved it, because it would piss Father off. Old Man Beckham picked up the can, spat and waited.

"Yes, sir. Is Miss Beckham in? My name is Regina and I'm with the Betts Community News. I wanted to interview Miss Beckham—I mean, I know it's a hard time right now, but I'd like to do a story if I can."

"Well, they gone over to the Branch to make arrangements." I knew the Branch, a longtime family owned funeral home. Father and Mother still went to them when needed. "You can talk to me. The boy was my grandson. I raised him from a pup." Beckham rubbed his thighs, opening up a little more. "Never knew his daddy—never did shit for him anyway. That's 'bout all you need to know."

"Uhh, sir, I was wondering if I could speak with his mother too, if that's possible. There's some questions that maybe only she can answer. Has anyone heard from the police or witnesses?"

"Hell, he was born and he died. What else you need to know? Yeah, he ran around with them dumb asses down the street. I tried to tell him go back to school. Get an education, do something with yourself. Just wouldn't listen. Told me I was old and stupid! That's all I gots to say."

Beckham picked up the Crisco can and spat again. I wrote notes in my mind as fast as I could. I could feel the breadth of Beckham's frustration. I decided not to press any further. "Thank you, sir. This sure helps. If his mother wants to talk, she can give me a call." I offered my card. One of the children took it, ran up the stairs and gave it to him. He took it without looking at me.

"Do what you want. That's how I feel." He spat into the can, lowered his hat over his eyelids and went into a sun-drenched sleep. The radio segued into a hard bop speaking his grandson's swift life. I went back to the office.

* * *

Three days later, Trinity and I met outside of Greater Progressive Baptist Church. A lot of people from the neighborhood turned out. I told Trinity about my talk with Beckham.

He listened, but I knew his mind was still on Lynn. I kept on running my mouth. "Wouldn't be surprised if Bryant showed up tonight."

Trinity dragged on his Kool and wiped his forehead. "Maybe. Maybe not. The superintendent's got him on the hot seat, burning his ass up. It'd help if they showed some concern. This is more than just a turf war."

We started across the street. I spied Lynn down the way on the corner, mixing with the wineheads. I wondered if she was hanging around, hoping that Trinity would see her.

The sanctuary was just as Trinity always described it when he would regale me with stories about being raised in this church. It used to be a Jewish temple before the war and the black migration from the south. The corner stone on the front still had its Hebrew inscriptions. It was cool inside the stone walls. Three large fans fought against the humidity gathering from the building crowd. We sat in the last few pews. I saw Old Man Beckham, whose pained face told a different story than the other day on the porch. Standing next to him, Miss Beckham cradled her other children.

We just sat and listened. I didn't want to see the body. I've never been much for funerals. Even with my own family, I only went out of obligation. Reverend Harris sat in the pulpit with two others ministers. Their black embroidered robes flowed just above the blue carpet. The other two preachers got up and pretty much said the same thing: to be strong and pray for the family. I heard but didn't hear. My mind drifted to how Trinity described he and Lynn's life in this church and how everything was not always singing and shouting. The small things, like the conversations he would have with his Daddy explaining everything in the world to a little boy. He told Trinity that the stained-glass windows came from the angels that God had sent down with coloring pencils to do his work. Even better was the story about how one of the pigeons would get in through the broken windows in the middle of a service and circle the heads of the deacon board. Trinity and the other Sunday school boys almost choked to death, trying not to burst out laughing and they'd take bets on whether one of the deacons would get anointed. The deacons would try in vain to shoo it away. After all these years, the windows were still broken.

I did feel weird, sitting and thinking those things in the middle of Reverend Harris' crowd stirring. He preached of faith and read from the Book of Job, explaining that all of this was a test and trouble don't last always and that Jesus said that time heals all wounds. I knew that to be true, but hearing Miss Beckham wail over her son the way she did, let me know that her healing had not yet begun. Reverend Harris used the double-edged sword parable, saying that pain and joy cannot be separated, though one might overtake the other sometimes and make us either laugh or cry. That when a bad spirit struts into our lives, it can make us crazy with pain, feeling like we are in the last vestiges of a storm.

The final closing of the casket gave us our clue to leave. I followed Trinity down the aisle, way behind the casket, Reverend Harris, the Beckhams and the other mourners.

When we stepped outside, there were still some remnants of an evening rain that had rolled in with clouds from the north. The air felt cooler, drying my make-up. As I waited for Trinity to unlock the car, I looked at Miss Beckham, familiar with her face—she was now one of those Mamas left to bear the burden.

I saw Lynn down the street, still hugging the corner. She stood long enough for me to see her, then disappeared cryptically. I gave Trinity a serious look. He knew I had something to tell. We would talk later. Maybe Lynn had something she wanted us to know—otherwise, she knew how to make herself invisible.

* * *

The phone calls started shortly after Beckham's funeral. It would ring. I would pick up, but no one answered. I tried not to get alarmed or anything like that. Jonas told me when he gave me my first op-ed column that sometimes people wouldn't like what I wrote. That they'd somehow get my unlisted number and this would be their way of saying *fuck you and your opinions*. It came with the territory. I knew my ideas were strong for a sister, but Angela Davis and Zora Neale Hurston had given me ammunition and I was going to shoot with both barrels. Father and Mother thought my job and Lawndale were equally dangerous and were the main reasons they wanted me back at home. I usually wasn't as worried as they thought I should be. My friends, Smith and Wesson, helped me sleep. But with the recent killings and all the secrecy with Sarge, my intuition was working overtime.

I could hear breathing on the other end. Sometimes when

they'd call, I'd try to elicit a response. "Listen, you sick motherfucker, you keep calling here, I'm going to report this to the phone company!" Then, I'd slam the receiver down. It didn't work because the calls started to become more frequent. I got the feeling that whoever was calling got a kick out of getting a rise out of me at three o'clock in the morning. I couldn't go back to sleep after the calls. So, I'd turn on the TV, lay back down and linger in the snowy-blue light until six. When I would come in to work after one of those nights, Trinity and Margret would notice. Jonas said nothing and couldn't care less. If Trinity tried to pry, I'd play it off and act like it was okay. But, the recent calls had started to bother me. It made me feel like someone was watching me, so I'd make sure when I undressed, I'd do it in the bathroom with the door closed. The only man who had ever seen my naked ass was Trinity and we'd always do it in the dark anyway. I even started to follow what Sergeant Bryant would say when he came to the block club meetings: to always walk on lighted streets, look behind you before putting your key in the door and never buzz anybody in if you weren't sure who they were. Most of the men on Roosevelt Road knew who I was and they knew that Trinity would bust their asses if they ever tried anything.

Trinity wasn't what you'd call a man of action in the tradi-tional sense, but he was a man who was quiet and didn't take no shit, especially when it came to me, Mama, Lynn and Malik. He had a reputation that spoke for itself, honest and forthright. It helped a lot when it came to Lynn's well-being. As drunk as she'd get sometimes, I can't ever remember hearing about some guy trying to take advantage of her like that. Not that there weren't any opportunities and it didn't help when Lynn put herself in harm's way.

* * *

One morning, Lynn had been on a binge and wound up nodding on a curve outside of the Pine Restaurant on 16th and Pulaski. It was autumn and the weather was changing. It was really chilly, even for Chicago's autumn air. Lynn pulled her fatigue jacket over her neck to fight off the chill. She was coming down off a high, giggling at her reflection in the puddle cradled in the sunken asphalt. She saw Sam draped in his dashiki. He reached out and Lynn took his hand. They stood at the stove in the rented kitchenette where they lived in college. The lamp on the table gave the ceiling a soft yellow glare. She and Sam danced a slow grind while Hendrix's guitar growled an angry blues.

Sam whispered and played with Lynn's earrings. "How's that boy doing down there?" He palmed her butt and pulled Lynn closer.

"How you know it's a boy?" Lynn licked his ear and buried her head in his shoulder. "Could be a mean sister kicking her way in. You never know."

"I know it's a boy. A man knows his stuff! When I say it's a boy, it's a boy."

"Yeah, but what if it's a girl? We all for equality and thangs, ain't we?"

"I get the point, baby. How about we have twins and..."

The sound of a car horn brought Lynn out of her nod. She jerked her head up and swung out with her fists. The driver's face looked familiar. *Liars are familiar*, Mama always said.

It was Andrew riding high in his purple Deuce and a Quarter. "Say, baby, what you doing out here in the rain?"

Lynn rubbed her eyes, trying to focus as Andrew's goodwill grin came into view. She wanted to ignore him but knew the pangs would come later like an equinox turning day into night and night into day. Maybe she could sucker him into giving her credit. Andrew knew she would be jonesing.

"Come on in out of the cold," Andrew waved. Lynn gave in.

Incense wafted through the open door as Lynn stepped into his car. She held onto the handle in case she needed to make a quick escape. Andrew hit the gas and headed east towards the rising sun.

Although Lynn had been in Andrew's basement what seemed like a million times, she stopped and surveyed the room like it was her first time. The dampness stuck to the bottom of her gym shoes as she walked across the floor over to the sunken couch. The bongo pops from the stereo's speaker changed Lynn's mood and she felt them even more when Andrew disappeared into the backroom. She knew he was in there cooking. She started to sweat more than usual. Lynn tried to bring herself back around, fixating on the door. A shadowy image of Sam took shape. He stood, palms up. Blood steamed from his face and puddled on the floor. Her heartbeat doubled and she grabbed her chest with one hand and rubbed her eyes with the other, hoping Sam would be gone when she lowered it. Each time she dared look, he was still there, bloodied hands outstretched. Before she knew it, Lynn had jumped up and headed out the door, stumbling up the concrete stairs, through the gate, staggering down the street.

Back in the basement, Andrew emerged from his lair with the works and a huge smile. "Alright baby. We gon' git it ..." He looked around. No Lynn. He reached back with his foot and kicked the door closed and flopped into his straw throne. He struck a match, held it under the spoon, threw his head back and forth, went into a nod mumbling to himself. "Sheeeit."

Lynn straightened her clothes and tucked in her shirt. She kept stumbling. She stopped herself long enough to hear Trinity's car horn. She tried to act like she didn't see him, but Trinity wouldn't budge. Their eyes locked and Lynn's shame won out. In a frenzied leap, she darted into the street and past the open car door and slumped into the seat. Trinity wiped her runny nose with a Kleenex like a father taking care of his baby. Lynn collapsed her head onto his shoulder and into his lap, sobbing. Trinity massaged her head the same way Mama used to when they were children. He held her hands, and for the first time, dared to look at her scars that made road maps along swollen thumbs and wrists and forearms.

* * *

Trinity's hard knocks on the door startled me and I reached under the couch for my gun. When I heard his voice, I jumped up and opened it. Trinity stood there holding up Lynn like a rag doll. He didn't have to say a word. I could see she was in pretty bad shape. She was the one who could make Trinity get up and leave my bed and my arms in the middle of the night with a call from Mama. The one I knew he was looking for when he'd stand and stare out the front window in silent repose, oblivious to me and everything else. When I looked at Lynn as he lay her on the couch and started to undress her, I wondered how someone who was as smart as her could be dragged down into an abyss like hers. It was what I wondered every day, when I first left Spelman, moved to Lawndale and started volunteering at a methadone clinic. Since 1970, they had been popping up all over Madison and Roosevelt at the community clinics along with a flood of money for hallway houses. My minor in college was psychology and helped me get the job at one of them, so I knew a little about the pangs of human behavior. I thought it would also help me in my writing and pursuit of journalism. I had witnessed and been directly involved in several detoxes. It wasn't a pretty sight. Trinity didn't say very much. He just hovered by the door looking like a lost sheep. I knew he wanted me to see if I could do something—anything to help. What would happen next was a roller-coaster of mood swings. After handing Lynn over to me, Trinity left.

Lynn was the blues. The kind that the old folks used to talk about in the kitchen when we were growing up. *You'll get them. Just keep on living. You'll get them. If you eat too much of them, they'll choke you and make your mouth too big for your stomach. Make us throw them back up. Ain't no escaping. We have to get the blues to learn. Learn how to waltz down that road. Learn how to sow our seeds. Learn how to hit that note that will carry us home.*

Lynn stopped whimpering and blacked out. She looked gaunt and drained. She could have been a corpse in the county morgue. It was close to five in the evening when she finally smelled herself. I dragged her to the bathroom several times. Her whole body ached every time she tried to sit up on her own.

"I heard about you," Lynn mumbled, trying to clear her throat. She made a feeble attempt to reach for a cigarette on my coffee table, but was stopped by her trembling hand. It just lay there looking at us.

I smiled, hoping it might help some. "Something good, I hope." I picked up the smoke and offered, but Lynn waved it off and rubbed her belly.

"I'll save it for later."

"It's okay, I understand. And what did you hear about me?"

"I hear things. I'm not totally out of it. If you're with Trinity, you must be okay."

"Glad you approve." I put the double locks on the door and watched her for any sudden moves. We sat in silence, studying each other. We were attached to the same man who had our hearts. Lynn broke the stalemate.

"I know Trinity well enough to know that any woman demanding his time has gotta be smart. He ain't never been no dummy. I taught him too well." A proud smile hid itself behind the lines on her face.

I relaxed a little bit. "He's a good man. He respects women. Treats me as an equal."

Lynn's head leaned to the side. "Had a man like that once. Trinity approved of him. Guess I haven't been around too much to approve of you."

I thought her gesture was heartfelt and softened a bit. "Guess not. But you're here now. He always spoke highly of you and Sam."

Lynn's eyes cleared. "Yeah. Too bad you didn't get to meet him. He got... uhh... he was..."

I held out my hand. She took it and I rubbed her scars. "It's okay, sister." Her face opened and her tears baptized it.

"Look, you know what's next." Lynn said. "What I'm gonna be up against. It's been a good while since I..." That thang had started to move on her. "...and I know you and Trinity trying to help and all..."

I interrupted. "But we don't know how it is."

Lynn's eyes darted. She licked her lips and picked at her face. "If I could ...just..."

"Sorry, sister. You ain't going nowhere. You know what you gots to do. I've seen it before." I tried to sound forceful, watching her draw her robe up against her chest and fight off the chills. I got up and stood by the door. It was coming.

Lynn rose unsteadily. "Seen it? Baby, you ain't seen shit! Living on Pill Hill! I know your family got money. I know who your daddy is. How he feel about you being around us po' folks?"

She kept edging towards the door. Twenty minutes ago, she was as weak as a newborn. But now that need was coming down on her and making her strong. I got ready for the humbug. She lunged at me. I fought back, grabbing her arms and spun her around. I hadn't forgotten the moves I learned at the clinic. She jerked backwards, slamming me against the door. I held on tight.

"Let me go, bitch! Let me go!"

"No can do. So settle down."

She kept trying to stamp my feet. We did a two-step for what seemed like forever, but I couldn't let go. She kept trying bite me, but I didn't care. I wouldn't let go. Beads of sweat rolled down her forehead. She was in her exodus and couldn't see a way out. "Okay. Okay, I give."

"Just be cool. You know you gon' have to let this shit pass. It ain't gon' be easy. Do it for your son. Do it for Mama. Do it for Trinity."

Her mind changed again. "Fuck them! Let me go! Let me go! Let me go!"

The pains of withdrawals had started. Lynn broke down and her sweat soaked through her robe. She shook and cried, growing weaker with every move. After about thirty minutes, she blacked out again, but not before throwing up her guts a second time. All I could do was hold her and pray. Rock her. Wipe her. And pray.

I managed to get out from under her, over to my bed and turned down the covers. Lynn lay by the door in a fetal position going through her rebirth. I kept the bucket on the side to catch what I could whenever the dragon roared and spit its flames. How Lynn let her life get so out of control perplexed me.

At the clinic, Lynn would be just another dark, listless, window-eyed junkie standing in line, waiting on a daily dose of methadone. Standing like the rest of them. On the outskirts, where society thought they should be. I knew that Trinity wanted to call, but I knew he wouldn't. I knew he feared Lynn wouldn't make it and wind up back on the same streets that plucked her heart strings with sour notes while she searched for peace.

Four days later, Trinity finally called. I was glad it was a Friday when he brought Lynn. I had to fake Jonas out with a sick day on Monday, because we only got two and I had used those up about a month ago. He was glad that Lynn had at least beat down her demon for a minute. We weren't sure how long it would last, but I had given my best efforts. She was still very weak though. She'd throw up the soup and water that I force fed her just to put something in her stomach. I didn't want her to get dehydrated. Then, we'd have a bigger problem on our hands. We talked about getting Lynn into one of the programs. I told Trinity, it would be better if it were a residential environment. Then, they could work on her behaviorally. If she was successful, then she could maybe move to the outpatient phase. Where she would stay then, I didn't know. He didn't know either. She damn sure couldn't stay with Mama and Malik. That would be a disaster. Whatever we decided, it would have to happen soon.

* * *

My friend Melanie said she had some hot news and I should know about it. News that even Sarge didn't want me to have. I nearly tripped over myself running out of the office. I had other connects in the department besides Sarge. When I couldn't get any response from him, I turned to Melanie. Whenever she called, I knew she had something good and juicy.

Melanie and I knew each other from way back in sixth grade. She was the daughter of one of the families in Maywood who was brave enough to welcome my family when we moved into the all-white neighborhood back in the early sixties. She was always a loose cannon, the way my Father looked at her. Trinity just loved her energy and honesty. She was radical and fearless to me. We went to a catholic high school and Melanie was always in trouble with the nuns who tried to tame her. She liked to smoke grass and loved music. Sometimes I would indulge with her. Then we'd kick back and down a few bottles of wine while I vented.

Her feminist views were shaped early on by her mother, who was an artist. Whenever I got into it with Father, she came to my aid when I needed someone to talk to. How Melanie got hired by the CPD, she never really let on. I would broach the question, but she always managed to change the subject and we'd end up talking about changing the system from the inside. I would accuse her of being a spy for some radical organization and then we'd fall out laughing. Melanie had settled down long enough to finish a paralegal program, so her parents were glad that she would be able to work. At the department, she was a kind of liaison between the police and the state's attorney office and had access to a lot of files a lot of other people didn't. A lot of that information was confidential.

"Girl, what's wrong? I've never seen you this nervous."

Melanie fumbled with several manila folders. "Gina. Gina. This is a bombshell!" She stopped at my car and dumped the folders onto the hood. I went inside the back seat and pulled out a large shopping bag and slid most of the folders into it. We stood, smoked and stared at each other, waiting for who would speak first. I figured that whatever was in those files had something to do with the murder of Old Man Beckham's grandson and the others. If nothing else, it was going to be dangerous. We decided to go to Red Hots across the street where they sold the Jew Town polish. It was a popular place inhabited by police, lawyers, judges, reporters and family members waiting on loved ones hanging on a bail or a verdict. With law enforcement, the major paper reporters were cool, but Betts was not looked at too kindly. We always put "a black slant on everything" At least that's how the superintendent put it to Trinity and Jonas when they had what they wanted to call a meeting. It was more like a shouting match, so I knew when some of those officers saw me and Melanie huddled together in a booth, it would get back to the brass right away, especially Sarge.

Melanie was breathless. "Gina, you won't believe it! You just won't believe it..."

She had me. "Believe what? What are you hiding?"

"You know that story you've been working on with the Beckhams?"

"Yeah?" I started to get a little irritated with Melanie's game. "Trinity and I are supposed to meet with his family later."

"Whoa! Well, after you see what I've got..."

"Melanie. Com'on, don't do this..." I pleaded.

She knew she had wetted my reporter's curiosity. Finally, she pulled two folders out of her purse just like the ones we dumped into the shopping bag. I grabbed a French fry and handled the edge of the folder, opening it like a vault full of gold. Copies of photos from the Beckham's boy crime scene. If this was original, then somebody manipulated the body before the crowd got there. Old Man Beckham's grandson was cut up in several places.

I discarded the fries and pushed the basket over to the side. "Jesus, Melanie. Where did you get these?"

"If I say that, then you become an accessory. You really want to know?" Melanie smiled, teasing me like a lover who won't let you cum right away. But this was a game we always played.

"Really!"

"Copped them while they were on the way to the Sarge's office. You know Sarge, don't you?" She smiled like a three-year-old smart enough to reach the cookie jar.

I knew I would have to decide whether I wanted to pursue this story, pulling Trinity and Melanie right along with me. What would happen if the Beckham family found out? It would tear them up even more than they already had been. It wouldn't be fair to do that to them.

We felt the gaze of the uniforms' suspicious eyes on us. I decided that we should cut it short and move on. I didn't want to say anything more to Melanie and I didn't want her saying anything more to me. We had already committed the crime. If we were ever questioned, then we'd have nothing to say. Sarge might forget his friendship with Father and have us arrested if he found out. I drew breath and we gave each other that look we always had since high school when it was time to scatter after we had done something foul and were feeling guilty. Those uniform eyes didn't help. We left separately. She left first while I sat pretending to read the Sun-Times. I waited until she made it out of the parking lot and back into the court house. Then, I slid the folders into my bag and tried to leave as inconspicuously as possible.

* * *

I got in my Pinto and headed straight for the Pine Restaurant on 16th and Pulaski to meet Old Man Beckham. The place had so much history on the Westside. In the 1950's and early 60's, blues players from B.B. King to Muddy Waters graced its stage. On each side of the Pine was a laundromat and cleaners. Father and Mother used to go there before we moved.

I caught a glimpse of Old Man Beckham through the large picture window framed in Christmas lights, sitting at the bar just as the jukebox cast its spell. The barmaid leaned across the bar, engaged in animated conversation with another patron. I walked in and the blue love song carried me over to him. Hopefully a scotch and soda would help cool my nerves, especially after seeing what Melanie had.

I took a seat next to him. "Mr. Beckham?"

"Hey young lady. How you doing?" I could tell he was a little tipsy. "Wasn't sure you'd make it." He looked down at his watch. Unlike before, he was a little more cordial, but the face of grief still pressed on his shoulders. "Let's make this quick, huh?"

"I know we didn't meet before under the best of circumstances. How is your family?" I ordered a JB and soda and went for my purse, but he waved me off and threw a ten on the counter. The barmaid cut her eyes at me, smiled and palmed it right away.

"Look, I ain't one to show no soft shoe, know what I mean?" Beckham said. "But something 'bout my grandson is bothering me that I ain't heard the police say."

I leaned forward and stirred my drink. I wondered what Beckham knew. Maybe he already knew what I had just found out. "Like what?"

"Like how Billy really died. He wasn't doing all that good, but he ain't done no much more bad than other people. He didn't deserve to get his throat slashed and cut up like that. Seemed like the morgue people tried to hide it when I went to claim the body. I don't know if my daughter will ever get over it."

He put his drink down hard. I pretended to catch my breath hoping that he wouldn't see through me. *You can't fool the old folks because the eyes don't lie.* "They slashed his throat?"

"Yeah. But it wasn't like they say. I been hearing things. People talk, y'know?"

"What things?"

"Like how it wasn't no they!" Beckham slammed his fist on the bar.

"Who then?"

"They say its one person and the police don't want it to get out. There's talk it's gonna be more. You got to stop it. Somebody got to stop this."

"Mr. Beckham, I've been doing some digging of my own. Just give me some more time. Please."

"Mam' all I got is time. My baby, she want to talk. Just told her about you coming by looking for her." Beckham finished his drink, threw a five on the counter, grabbed his hat and left. I sat and listened to the jukebox's sailing drum solo. If there ever was the blues, Old Man Beckham had them. The scotch had started to sour in my stomach. That's what I get for drinking so early in the day. I thought about Billy and what happened to him. Might as well left that boy on a slave ship in the Atlantic and waved goodbye.

* * *

Two days later, Trinity and I pulled up in front of the Beckham place. As we sat, I took in his cologne and rubbed his thigh. He kissed me lightly on my cheek. It wasn't a romantic kiss, but one of reassurance. We had talked most of the night before. I told him about the photos from Melanie, my talk with Beckham and my suspicions. He told me about his encounter with Funkee in front of Andrew's basement and the man in blue business. We decided that there might be something to that, but neither of us knew for sure. The one thing we did know was that we were going to have to walk through this fire together, like God used fire to mold His people. Well, we weren't Moses and certainly weren't Jesus, but we knew that this whole thing could get very hairy and the skeletons could fall out of the closet and on top of us all if we kept on probing.

Old Man Beckham wasn't sitting out front this time. Several children played in the yard. We approached the tall, gray frame, stepped through the gate and onto the concrete trail that led to the garden apartment. The door was open behind the screen. One of the kids ran into the apartment and Miss Beckham came out. She had a short and slender but sturdy frame. Her hair was braided in a circle on top and then flared into afro puffs. She wore a dashiki, jeans and sandals. For a woman who had birthed four kids, her body had still not given in to her age. I imagined her in a cotton field—bending and stooping with a child strapped to her back. Her face spoke love, sacrifice and devotion. Her devotion was to her children. Now she had given one back to the universe. The other three were hers to keep.

She squinted into the sun behind us. "Can I help you?"

Then Old Man Beckham stepped into the doorway. "It's alright, baby. This is the woman I told you about. Let 'em in."

Miss Beckham turned and looked at him. "Well, com'on in." She was already halfway in the door. I walked behind

Trinity, stopped and went into my purse. The kids sensed the peppermints and crowded around me. Inside, Miss Beckham offered us coffee and went into the kitchen, a few steps away from the living room. It was a clean, modest home. Pictures adorned the walls. A copy of Billy's obituary laid on the coffee table blessed by an angelic porcelain statuette. I introduced Trinity to Mr. Beckham and waited for his approval. I explained that sometimes we work together to watch each other's backs.

Old Man Beckham nodded satisfaction, so I relaxed. He gestured towards Trinity. "Saw you at the funeral, young blood. You was sitting in the back. I figured you was with her. Heard anything more about Billy?"

Miss Beckham returned with the cups and poured the brew. She reached for Old Man Beckham's cup, but he waved her off. He reached down, came up with a half pint and refilled his cup.

Miss Beckham shook her head and shot him a look before she began. "Miss Gina, I ain't blaming nobody for the way Billy died. He was hard-headed, I know. Quitting school. Mixing in with the wrong crowd and things. But that didn't make him no bad person. I loved him all the same. At the morgue, I guess he looked so bad, Daddy didn't even let me see him. Whatever it was they did to him, he didn't deserve that! When I finally went over... over to Branch, he say he did the best that he could. What did they do to my boy?" Her eyes glazed over. She dropped her cup on the table, got up went to answer the call of the coffee pot she had left on the stove. I followed her into the kitchen.

I wanted to reach out and hug her, but remembered what Jonas had always told us about interviews. No matter how emotional they get, never touch them. It would only shade the objectivity you need to bring to the story. I didn't have any kids—or even nieces and nephews—but somehow I still felt a kinship. We came from two different worlds. I had never known what it was like to have a welfare check or the sting of an angry, overly-suspicious case worker. Even so, we still stood on common ground. The common ground of color. We still got the same stares from security in the downtown department stores. We went back into the living room with Old Man Beckham and Trinity.

"So what are you saying, young blood? This cat might be putting these boys out of their misery like they ain't going to grow up anyway?" Old Man Beckham's hand trembled. His cup banged the glass table and the scotch puddled. He stumbled through the screen door into the yard and headed for the fence gate. The children scattered as he bobbed and weaved and turned his head up to the sun. He leaned over the gate, trying to hide his grief, but his heaving shoulders gave way.

Miss Beckham got up and moved to the window to part the curtains. A wind had picked up. Hot and humid, it wafted and stirred through the room like a restless spirit shutting out the noise in the yard. The sunlight whispered and moaned, trying to soften the room, but gray clouds loomed.

"You know he might act like he hard and all that, but what happened is tearing him up," she said solemnly. "He raised that boy. Billy's other brothers and sisters, no, they ain't going that way. I'll move south before I let the streets take them. We ain't never had much. But I try to give everything I got to those kids. Daddy helps with his pension. But I be off work so much... shoot, we practically live off it. Nobody around here starving though. My Mama told me a long time ago before Billy was born, that with boys, especially black boys, *you better get ready.* No matter how those words come to me lately it still hurts deep." She wiped her tears.

Pregnant clouds gathered like they do on Friday evenings in the summer. Come morning, somebody else's mother would be crying. The wind moved the curtains again. A storm was brewing and I was in the midst of it. Old Man Beckham flicked his cigarette butt into the gutter while that same wind baptized him. A storm was brewing and the Beckhams were in the midst of it. They were the beasts carrying the burdens.

* * *

On the drive back to the office, Trinity finally let me in on what he had been holding back. It was about Funkee and Lynn. I got excited, but tried not to show it. We hadn't seen Lynn since the evening I came home and saw my door left wide open. I didn't trip. Neither did Trinity. He was slowly coming to an acceptance about Lynn and her life. I know it was hard and tearing him up, but the truth was the truth. In her own way, Lynn was helping us. We just didn't see it right then. She was communicating with us through Funkee. I think she was too embarrassed and her pride—assuming she still had some—wouldn't let her face us right now.

Trinity was cruising around. He was quiet, which was not that unusual, but I made a point not to disturb him. The cool air after a rain had brought out some people onto their porches. They sat listening to their radios, enjoying themselves. We rounded the corner on Douglas and Millard, heading north towards Andrew's house of horror. He was still wearing the same dingy, dirty clothes when Trinity had seen him last. Trinity slowed the car. Funkee was about to run, but recognized that we weren't plainclothes or someone he had stolen from, looking to kick his ass. Funkee stopped and smiled, breaking out into his pee-pee dance. It was as if he knew that Trinity would have to come back to him in need. We got out of the car and walked towards him.

"I was wondering... y'know, man..."

"Wondering what? When I'd come back?" Trinity lit a Kool and offered me one. I took it. Then, he offered one to Funkee. He reached out with an unsteady hand. I looked at all the dirt lodged between his nails. Vitiligo and burned skin graced the rest.

"Look, let's cut through the chase." I could see Trinity's growing impatience already. I knew Trinity hated that Lynn had sent Funkee with information. "What you said before...?"

Funkee smiled. The devil played at his lips as he dragged his smoke. "Baby blue?"

"Yeah, yeah. Baby blue—what'd you mean by that?" Trinity asked, speaking through his own smoke.

"Well, y'know, y'know, y'know..." Funkee looked away and scratched his head. His hand reached in and out of his pocket, reaching for nothing and coming back with nothing.

"Okay. Will this do?" Trinity fished in his pocket and came up with a ten. He held it out between his middle and index finger, careful not to touch him. Funkee snatched it and pocketed it right away. I sensed Funkee was already feening his next hit. Then, Trinity widened his stance and discarded his smoke in case he had to drop him if he tried to run off. "What'd you see?"

"Weird stuff, man. Weird stuff," Funkee waved his arms like a magician finishing his trick. "It'd blow your mind, see. That is if you ain't used to it."

Trinity played along. "Yeah. Yeah."

"I was in the alley."

"What alley?"

"13th and Millard. Behind where your Mama stay. Me and

Lynn."

Our ears opened up. "Lynn?"

"We was looking for some things, y'know? Then we heard it."

"Heard what?"

"The boy. He was knocking him to the ground. Then he pushed him into the trunk."

"Trunk? What kind of car was it? License plates?"

"It was dark. He didn't have no lights. I think it was black, like a plainclothes ride, but it didn't have no antennae on top." Funkee wiped his nose. Time was running out. The ten was burning a hole in his pocket.

"Did you or Lynn hear anything? Anything at all?"

"Nothing. Nothing. But he had on a uniform."

"What kind of uniform? Com'on, man... fess up!"

"Y'know—what they wore when we was kids. Same blue as now. But old, y'know?"

"Then what happened?"

"I don't know. Hid our asses behind the cans. We didn't want no trouble." Trinity gave him another Kool. Funkee lit it and dragged hard. "He closed the trunk and drove real slow like he was trying not to make no noise. Then, he disappeared on 13th."

"What'd you and Lynn do?"

"Shit, we got the fuck outta there! What would you do? We knew it was a body he was handling. Sho' weren't no garbage. That's all she told me to tell you when I saw you."

"One more thing."

"What? What, man? I got business to take care of." Funkee's whole body was leaning towards Andrew's basement down the street.

"Where's Lynn?"

"Don't know. Don't know." Funkee side-stepped us and took

off.

I know that it made Trinity feel a little better hearing that Lynn was somewhere out there alive. Maybe not well, but at least alive. For all we knew she was watching us now, making sure Funkee made contact with us. Lynn was like that. We got back in my Pinto and rode around the corner onto Roosevelt Road, heading to the office.

There, I took a long deep breath and settled back into my chair letting the events of the previous days sink in. Just when I thought I could relax, the phone rang. It was Mother. She sounded worried. She told me that Sarge and Father had been conferencing in his office all morning and when they came out, neither looked too happy. Father told her to call me and let me know that Sarge wanted to talk to me ASAP. After talking to Mother, I made like I was going to the bathroom, so Trinity didn't worry or wonder what was up. He didn't deserve the heat that I knew was coming. He already had his family to worry about. I slid out of the door when I thought Trinity was taking his ten-minute nap ritual. I told Margret to tell him that I had to go see about something for Mother if he asked.

* * *

I thought we'd be meeting alone, but Sarge's office was full with two uniformed officers, another sergeant and a lieutenant. My reporter's instincts raced with my mind around the room, stopping to take mental snapshots of everyone there. I knew it must be serious. Probably about the copies of those goddamn files Melanie gave me. I was praying, *Lord let them be just copies and not the originals* or I was surely going to jail.

They all sat quietly looking at me, waiting for me to break

down or make the first move. I clutched the arms of my chair, opening and closing my fingers to let the air dry the sweat attempting to seep out and drip. I desperately wanted to light up a Kool but wouldn't dare. It would confirm whatever suspicions they already had.

Sarge had probably told Father that this meeting was going to take place and he had to make sure that he played his role as a professional or his job would be on the line. He broke the ice, speaking like an attorney and I was on the witness stand. "Miss Foster, do you understand that we aren't accusing you of anything? We just want some clarity."

I played along and made sure to sit up straight and keep eye contact. "About what?"

"Young lady, don't play games with me." The coldness in his voice had just the right tone, the kind that might take away any suspicions the other people in the room might have about Father's and Sarge's relationship.

"Games? The Olympics are two years away."

Sarge smiled and leaned back in his leather chair, knowing that we had connected. "So you don't deny that you and your acquaintance, Melanie... I mean, Miss Ireland... met this morning at the restaurant across the street?"

"I don't deny knowing her, but lots of people eat there."

"Did you meet with her or not?"

I wasn't stupid. I knew some of those officers standing there like vultures had probably seen us in the booth, "Yes, I saw her, I see her all the time! Why are we here? Don't you meet people for lunch at work sometimes?"

"Yes, but not to ask me to steal." Sarge leaned forward and pointed his finger.

"Steal? And what was it I was supposed to have stolen?

"Did Miss Ireland give you any files?"

"Files? What files? I'm sure Melanie handles files all day long. I imagine it's a part of her job. Right?"

"The files on the Beckham case. And maybe others."

"Beckham? Hmmm… he was the one found murdered the other week, right?"

"So, you admit you handled some files on the case."

"I'm not admitting anything. You can surmise what you want. Unless you charge me with a crime, I can meet with whomever I please, wherever I please. This is a free country. I see you haven't checked your file cabinet lately. If these so-called files were missing, couldn't you just check your cabinet?" I motioned over to the far wall.

"And you say that they are in the cabinet over there? Are you sure?"

"Look, I didn't say shit. What you keep in your cabinet is your own business. If these files are that important, I'd surely keep them in a safe place."

"Like a file cabinet in my office?"

"Uh, yeah. Like a file cabinet in *my* office."

"Okay. So let's just take a look." Sarge motioned towards one of the officers standing. He went over to the cabinet, unlocked it and reached in the drawer. His hand emerged with several thick folders. He brought them over to Sarge's desk and stood there, anticipating the firestorm. He even reached back for his handcuffs. Sarge thumbed through the folders and reared back in his chair with an exasperated look on his face. He closed the last folder, restacked them and shoved the pile over to the side.

"You think you're pretty smart, don't you?"

"Well, sir, I did do some college, y'know?"

Sarge blew up. "Listen, young lady, we've already spoken to

your father! He knows you're skating on thin ice. And if we find that you and your friend have been tampering with these files—well, you know for yourself, that's a criminal offense."

"First of all, my Father doesn't have anything to do with this. Second, anything you accuse me of, you better be able to prove it. That's all I know."

"I'm well aware of what I have to prove. As for your father, he's a pillar of the community. But you, you, you…"

"You what?" I shot back. "Go ahead and say it."

"This meeting is over. I'll tell you one last thing before you go."

"What's that?" I asked, rising from my seat.

"Watch your step, young lady—*watch your step!*"

Sarge's warning hit hard, but the collusion between him and Father hit even harder. I knew Father was sitting in his office again, smiling to himself behind his great mahogany desk, knowing all along what had just transpired. Sarge would probably be on the phone with him as soon as I left.

I half turned and balanced on my heels. "Are you finished?"

"For now," Sarge said, swiveling away to look out of the window.

I carefully maneuvered my way past the other people in the room and into the hall. I didn't feel good at all. I relaxed my stomach and let out the gas that had been beating down the door the past half-hour. I had to admit I was a little shaken this time. This case was much too explosive to make any mistakes, especially a mistake like that. If it blew up here, it could blow up out in the streets. That would be the worst thing that could happen.

Three years after King's assassination and they still hadn't repaired Roosevelt Road, 16th Street and other areas in Lawndale.

Nothing left to tear down. I knew Sarge had to put me on a skewer and throw me on the burners in front of the very people who would report what had just gone down to his bosses. He wasn't going to put his job and career on the line, and I shouldn't expect him to do that. That'd be too presumptuous. I couldn't take advantage of him like that. His heart was in the right place. I would deal with Father later.

* * *

On the way back to the office, I took Roosevelt Road heading towards Central Park. The Pinto had done alright so far. When I rounded the corner at Central Park, it got sick on me and started coughing and smoking from underneath the hood. I steered over to the curb, got out cursing and leaned on the roof. I fanned the rising smoke and wondered how I was going to get this thing down the alley to Mitch's garage. I stood there trying to calm myself down when I heard Malik's voice. He was coming out of the mouth of the alley with his friends Calvin and John, doing what eleven-year-old boys do in the summer. Boy, was I glad to see them.

"Hey Miss Gina," Malik said, already understanding the charm of his smile.

"Hey, Malik. Wow, I'm glad to see you." I needed help, but played coy.

"Looks like you need some help. Uncle T told me if I ever see you and you need some help..."

He didn't have to finish. "Well, you see my problem."

He and his friends walked around to the front and opened up the hood, scrutinizing like surgeons that were going to cure a patient's pain. But all they did was hold up the hood and let out the rest of the smoke.

Malik was sharp and read my mind. "Mr. Mitch's garage is right on the other side of Millard down there." He pointed west down the alley. "We can..."

I patted my purse. "I'll pay what I can."

Malik looked at Calvin and John. I got in while they ran around to the trunk and started using all of the young muscle they had. I tried my best to avoid the broken glass, potholes and smashed cans. The last thing I needed was a flat. The sun was at its highest point and those boys were pushing with all their might. In the rear-view mirror, I could see their soaked T-shirts and brown arms.

We finally crossed Millard Street and Mitch heard my tires crunching debris and came out of his garage. He stood wide-legged with his hands on his hips. He steered us into his garage and we got as close to straight as we could without hitting the other car. When I got out, the boys were already lined up with their hands out. I gave them what I could. Before I turned around to talk to Mitch, they were already running down the alley to Joe's for ice cream and penny candy.

"Laid out on you again, huh, Miss Gina?" Mitch's hand circled his beer belly under his grease-splotched shirt. Mitch was like a second father to Trinity, so he knew me well.

"Yeah, Mr. Mitch, I'm hoping that it may not be done." I gave him my best damsel-in-distress look. "Can you work your magic for me one more time?"

"Like anything else, miracles cost money, Miss Gina." His head was already under the hood.

When he worked, Mitch talked nonstop, always bringing up stories about Trinity's daddy and himself. I listened to his wisdom. His portable radio was always tuned to WVON, known as the *Black Giant* in the community. It had been the eyes, ears and voice of the community for years since it broadcast one of the first call-in live interviews with Martin Luther King Jr. That night, they received so many calls, it forced Ma Bell's phone company to create a 591 exchange for talk radio. If Mitch didn't hear about on 'VON, then it wasn't true as far as he was concerned.

Mitch, his wife Cora and Trinity's Mama and Daddy had all followed the migration out of Mississippi after World War II and headed for Chicago's Westside. Mitch and Daddy met and served in Korea. During the war, they became like brothers. Both of them were from the south and had grown up under the hand of the segregation, spawned by the civil war. Mitch always regaled me with stories about what it like for blacks moving from the south to the north—why some stayed and why some fled to Chicago. The whole rundown. I sat on one of the milk crates Mitch used for chairs and listened to his first-hand history.

Mitch reached without looking and found a wrench in his tool box and went into one of my favorite stories about him and Trinity's daddy. They could argue about the strangest things, but it was what cemented their blood bond. I will never forget him telling me about the time Trinity's Daddy stopped by to pick up his car. They had been drinking since early morning while Mr. Mitch was finishing his work. The gin had given Daddy its devilment, so he was looking to hit a nerve.

"You looking for something?"

"Say, Mitch, where'd that hole come from?"

"What hole? What you talking about, man?"

"This hole right here," Mitch looked puzzled, raised his hand and scratching his head as Trinity's daddy pointed.

"Don't know. Maybe it was already there."

"Weren't there when I brought it in. No sir."

"Bullshit! You accusing me of putting it there?"

"I ain't accusing you of nothing. I'm just saying..."

"Saying what?" Daddy steadied his left leg, ready to throw a punch with his right fist. "Don't be calling me no liar, especially 'round my boy."

The whole thing had spun out of control. An adolescent argument fueled by alcohol and a summer's heat. It always ended with Trinity motoring out of the garage, across the grass and up the steps into the house where Mama and Cora were cooking. They'd come out spitting fire and brimstone hollering about how stupid two grown men looked, arguing in front of a boy. They women told them they had better calm down and find some common ground to stand on. When I pressed Trinity about where that hole actually came from, he'd laugh and shrug his shoulders and look at me like as if to say *don't ask stupid questions*. It was never anything bad enough that another cold Bud and a shot of gin couldn't resolve.

Underneath these stories were lessons about color and society. Listening to Mr. Mitch's descriptions gave life and made them real. In the army, Mitch and Trinity's Daddy were inseparable. They could be at each other's throats, and in the next second, be as tight as hand and glove. Mr. Mitch took pride in telling me about their army days.

Mitch came out from under the hood, pouring sweat. He picked up one of his handkerchiefs laid on the clean table and started to wipe his brow. I don't know how he could stand the work in this heat at his age.

"Look, I got work to do. You eating up my time. It should up and running one more time, Miss Gina." Mitch slammed the hood down. "But you know, maybe you might want to think about investing in another before you get stranded someplace you ain't got no business." Mitch reached down and grabbed another cold one from the cooler.

"Yeah. I know. Got to find some funds." I leaned on the hood. "With what they pay me at Betts, it's hard."

"Heard you been working overtime, Miss Gina. They ain't paying you for that?"

"Overtime? Just working on a story as usual. Where'd you hear that anyway?"

"I hear things. Just concerned is all. Asking too many questions can get you in trouble sometimes. Just make sure you ask the right people. Tell the truth, it's what they say about those murders. They ain't kosher."

I wondered if he had talked to Trinity or Old Man Beckham, who was much closer in age. "What makes a murder kosher? A murder is a murder as far as I know." I gripped the door handle and waited for Mitch advice.

"It ain't kosher when it's one of your own. Kinda like when me and Trinity's Daddy was in Korea. One time... well, they sent this nig—uh, Negro... from Alabama or somewhere..."

"Y'all didn't like him because he was from Alabama?"

"Wasn't that we didn't like him. He didn't like us. At least the dark-skinned niggers like me and Trinity's Daddy—called us darkies, tar babies and whatnot, just like the white folks. See, he was high yellow and color struck as the day is long."

"Oh, wow!" I leaned back and hit the grease-stained wall before jerking forward.

"I hauled off and hit him dead in the mouth one day."

"What did he say, Mr. Mitch?"

"Told me to clean the latrines."

"That's pretty common in the service, isn't it?"

179

"Not if you ain't got supplies, it ain't. And like I say, he rode me and Trinity's Daddy for the way we looked, not because we was lazy."

"So, what's your point?"

"You been to college, ain't you, Miss Gina? Uniforms? One of your own?" Mitch scoffed at me and drained his Budweiser and threw the can in the barrel with the rest of the empties. Mitch was really trying to tell me something about the story I was working on. I'm sure he had heard about what we had so far from Trinity. But Mitch would say no more. He left it to me to figure it out.

"What do I owe you for the work?"

"Tell Trinity to see me." Mitch winked at me and turned away. He opened the door. I got in, started it up and backed out into the alley. I waved and headed towards the street.

About the Author

Terry Clark lives and works in Chicago. His publications include several short stories with *Rigorousmag*; *The New Scriptor Journal*; *Taj Mahal Review*; *Art & Prose*; *Timbooktu* and *poeticdiversity*.